Treasure Box

Andrea Lige-Saddler
Published By: Risk and Rise

"When you lie to me and I know; I give you the opportunity to tell the truth, but you don't. Those continual lies are the stepping stones that you build, which will make it easier for me to walk away from you."

- Andrea Lige-Saddler

CONTENTS

Acknowledgements

I must take the time to thank my husband for always supporting me. To my four sons, thank you for being patient with me. To all my bookers', thank you! There are too many of you to single out, but there is one that always encouraged me to complete this sequel to my first novel "Project Whore" and that is La'Tera Guy, who also happens to be my niece. I also have to give a huge thank you to Skyy So'Journer Gaulden for editing my book. Jessica O'Dell is the world's best event coordinator, thank you so much. A thank you to the most important person in my life and that would-be God, please continue to use me and guide me in everything that I do.

1 NEW BEGINNING

"Keysha's been stabbed! Keysha's stabbed!" Monique began to scream.

Harmony came running into the room to see her mother holding the phone in her hand. She was hanging off the smoke grey leather sofa sobbing.

"Mom! Mom! "She yelled.

"What is wrong?" Harmony put her hands on her mom's shoulder.

Monique could not have mouthed the words to speak. She just sat there in disbelief. She let the phone fall from her hands and was staring out into space. Monique looked around her house; from the floor to the wall glass windows. The artwork was gorgeous. She was living like a queen, but would give all this up to make sure her cousin would be ok. Monique finally heard her daughter yelling in the background.

"Mom, what happened? I'm going to call Xavier." She said.
"No baby don't call him, he can't help me anyway." Monique looked up.
"What is wrong" She looked scared.

"Your aunt Keysha was stabbed pretty bad today at the jail and they don't know if she is going to make it."
"What?!" She slowly sat down.
"I know; my best friend could be gone." She began to cry again.
"Mommy I am so sorry. Even though I didn't know that much about Auntie Keysha, I know how much you two loved each other."
"I will never hear her voice again." Monique's voice trembling.
"We have to be optimistic that she will be ok. We have to tell Treasure and Grandma." Harmony sighed.
"I haven't even thought about that."
"I will go to the hospital to tell Treasure and you can tell Grandma. Trust me, you are not alone. I got your back and your front mom. I love you."
Monique chuckled, "I got yours too and I love you even more."
She kissed her forehead. "Which hospital again?"
"Mercy General." She said
"Mom, you know Treasure is working there today. I have to go now." She began to rush.
"I didn't even think of that. Try and get there before the ambulance." Monique jumped to her feet.
"On it mom, see you at the hospital."
Harmony got up, walked out of the family room and into the huge foyer where there was an oversized round table where she always threw her keys. She picked them up and headed out the door to the hospital to tell

Treasure the horrible news. She wasn't sure how she would respond but she loved her so it didn't matter. Monique wasn't far behind her, hoping her mother would be okay. It hadn't been that long ago that she lost her only sister, whom she was on extremely bad terms with at the time of her death.

"God give me the strength to deal with this day." Monique took a deep breath and closed the door. Treasure was sitting in the ER. The emergency room waiting area is full of vomiting adults and sick children. It made her nauseous; she wanted to work for herself, not cleaning up bodily fluids. As she was about to enter the next patients room she checked her light blue scrubs for everything she needed. She stuck her hand in her pocket. A pen, Band-Aids and stethoscope around her neck. Treasure wasn't a nurse, but a nursing tech. She called it doing grunt work, while the nurses got paid the big bucks to delegate jobs for her to do. She entered the room.

"Mrs. Nickels?" Treasure tried to sound upbeat.

"Yes, that's me." She put on a smile.

"What brings you in today?"

"Why do you people come in here asking the same damn question every time you come in here?" Looking annoyed.

Ms. Nickels was a black homeless woman who was beaten up by some young girls on the street. She really looks good to be homeless Treasure thought. She had really beautiful light brown skin, with her hair in a bun and white straight teeth. Treasure wondered if she was really homeless.

"Ms. Nickels I just need to understand what happen so I can properly access you." Treasure smiled.

"Some young dumb girls beat me up trying to steal my Michael Kors bag." She rolled her eyes.

Now Treasure was definitely taken by surprise. How the hell she can afford a Michael Kors bag if she's homeless? Treasure was at the point where she could care less. She was on her fourth night of doing a 12-hour shift. She just couldn't put her finger on that one. Just at that moment Dr. Nyugen walked in.

Dr. Nyugen was a Philippians doctor and gorgeous to say the least. He was about 5'11 which was very unusual for his nationality Treasure thought. It didn't matter, he was sexy and she didn't discriminate against anyone. He caught Treasure staring at him.

"Treasure who do we have here?" The doctor asked.

"We have Miss" Treasure was about to finish when she was interrupted.

"I can speak for myself! You have Miss Nickels, as in NOT married." She flirted.

Treasure began to chuckle just a little. Dr. Nyugen gave her a look to show is distaste in her unprofessionalism. She quickly got herself together and started to put her gloves on to take the bandages off Miss Nickels wounds.

"Well Miss Nickels, how are you doing?" He smiled at her.

"Great since you came in here." She flashed those pearly whites.

Treasure stood in the corner, while the doctor conducted his assessments. She couldn't help but look at Miss Nickels and think about her own mother. She decided right then and there she would go see her this weekend. She loved her mother and the talks on the phone and letters just weren't enough. She loved her Aunt Monique, but she wasn't her mother. Her mother's struggles made her very determined in life to be a true boss and take no shortcuts. As for her father Davon, she could care less about a man who infected her mother with HIV on purpose to end her life in such a painful way. She told herself she would never go see him.

"Treasure could you please get Miss Nickels some ice water and graham crackers." He ordered.

She was so irritated by the condescending way he said it to her. She hated her job and was thinking about the job her Uncle Xavier offered her. She figured it had to be way better than this bull shit.

"Of course." She faked a smiled.

"Also, I want a small amount of ice in the cup." She smirked.

"I got you Miss Nickels and I hope you choke on the ice." She whispered.

"Okay Miss Nickels, I will check on you in little while." Dr Nyugen waves at her as he leaves.

"I sure hope so." She laughed and began to cough. "I think I need that water STAT Treasure. Treasure rolled her eyes.

This bitch is really tripping. Treasure walks up the hall to get the water and crackers, thinking about how much she hates this job. She hated the hours, the nasty attitudes and most certainly, the pay.

"Excuse me Treasure, can I see you for a minute please." He motioned her into an empty patient's room. What now Treasure was thinking. I am so tired of this hospital. Do this, get that and that's your job.

"Can it wait until I get Miss Nickels water and crackers?" She asked

"No, it can't, Leslie can you get some water and crackers for Room 25 please?"

"Of course I can? She smiled.

Leslie was such an ass kisser. She was in her late forties and still trying to be a thot. She had a gold tooth, bright as the sun with blonde thinning hair and red lipstick. Leslie gave her that "your ass in trouble again" look. Treasure had been written up several times for speaking her mind or as the hospital would say being unprofessional.

"Could you have a seat please?" He asked.

He began to pull the curtain and leaned up against the door. He looked up at the ceiling and sighed. He folded his arms and began to tap his foot.

"What?" She said.

"What is exactly it?" He looked at her.

"I haven't done anything today." She smiled at him. He could not resist Treasure beautiful smile. This woman was gorgeous. He looked at her long brown hair with light brown under tones, beautiful green eyes and flawless skin. If it wasn't for her sharp tongue and speak your mind mouth she would be perfect.

"They want to fire you." He said.

"Fire me for what?!" She stood up.

"Treasure you are so unprofessional in the way you speak at times; you need to work on that." He looked at her.

"Okay so because I don't take anyone's shit, I'm a target?" She said.

"That's exactly what I'm talking about. Like what you just said in Miss Nickels room. I heard you and you're lucky it was me or tonight would have been your last night here." He stared at her. "It's your mouth. How do you say it? Just ratchet." He smiled.

Treasure started walking towards him. She was so close, that her stethoscope was pressed up against his stomach.

"You mean this mouth?" She kissed him.

He was enjoying every moment of Treasure kissing him. He started to feel warm and his dick began to press against his pants. He grabbed her and started rubbing on her butt. They were both groaning and moaning.

"Do you want to fuck me on this bed like you did last night?" she asked him.

"Yes, but there are no locks on this door, luckily we did not get caught last time." Breathing heavily.

"That's the exciting part about it." She said quietly as she licked his neck.

"You are going to make me lose my license fucking with you." He smiled.

He turned the lights off and pushed Treasure backwards towards the bed. He stuck his fingers down her scrubs and began fingering her. She began to moan because she knew his dick was huge and she needed that release.

"Code Blue Room 25. Code Blue Room 25." A voice said over the hospital intercom.

"Code Blue. Code Blue Room 25," The voice said once again.

Dr. Nyugen and Treasure looked at each other and ran out of the room and to Miss Nickel's room. When they got there another attending physician and the charge nurse was in the throes of performing CPR. They were doing everything to save her. It was chaotic, everyone moving at warp speed. It was about bad, really bad.

"Dr Nyugen we have an ambo coming in from the jail, victim has been stabbed multiple times and is also HIV positive arrival time is two minutes." The nursed yelled.

"Okay, Treasure you come with me and you guys keep working on Miss Nickels."

Treasure was feeling so uneasy about this night. It's crazy but not this crazy. She was moving just as fast as everyone else. She grabbed her gloves, mask and gown because the patient is HIV positive. They went and stood in the shock trauma room. Just in the nick of time, because the EMT's are rolling her in.

"Patient name is Keysha, in her late thirties, HIV positive, been stabbed multiple times, BP 75/50. She's in really bad shape." He said.

"Treasure." Dr Nyugen called her.

"Treasure." The nurse said.

Treasure ran out of the room and went into the grieving room. She could not believe it. The patient was her mother! Tears ran down her face. She started thinking about all the times she skipped out on going to see her and cutting her phone calls short. Treasure sat back in the chair feeling like she was having a panic attack, when Dr Nyugen walked in.

"What the hell is wrong with you?" He said. "Treasure what is wrong with you?!?! I think I'm going to have to let you go."

Treasure lifted her head up and tears were coming down her face. They stood there in shocked, because Treasure never showed and emotions at work like this.

"The HIV patient is my mother." She said

They all just stood there in silence. Dr. Nyugen asked the charge nurse to leave. He shut the door and pulled her into his arms.

"How is she?" she asked him.

"It's bad but we think she will make it." He said.

"What about Miss Nickels?" Treasures asked him

"She didn't make it. She too was HIV positive, but her heart just gave out."

"What is going to happen to my mom?"

"When and if she recovers, she will be sent back to jail."

"She can't go back there. I have to help her."

"Theirs is nothing you can do about it."

"Oh yes there is and you're going to help me." She demanded.

He looked confused. How could he help her stay out of jail? There was a knock at the door.

"Treasure your family is here." The Charge nurse said.

They all came in hugging and crying. Not knowing exactly what to expect but hoping for the best.

"Dr. Nyugen this is my Aunt Jackie, Aunt Monique and my cousin Harmony who you know already."

"Hi, can you please tell us what happened?" Monique asked

"Well Keysha came by ambulance and had multiple stab wounds to her body, she lost a lot of blood."

"Is she okay?" Jackie cried.

"Well……" He said.

"She's gone." Treasure said. "She didn't make it."

"What, she's gone?" Jackie screamed.

"My poor cousin." Monique grabbed her chest.

Her aunt Jackie passed out, Monique started crying. Dr. Nyugen was attending to her aunt and looked up at Treasure as she was being consoled by Harmony. He didn't know why Treasure told her family her mom was dead when she actually wasn't. What was she planning to do? He was finally able to get Jackie up and sat her down.

"Ma'am are you okay?" He asked.

"No, I'm not. My poor niece she just could never catch a break." Jackie cried.

"Mom it's going to be okay. We will be okay." Monique hugged her.

"Come here Treasure, I'm so sorry baby." Jackie just held her.

"Mom why isn't Treasure crying." Harmony asked.

"It's a lot to take in we all grief differently." Monique explained.

"Well I want to see her." Jackie stood up.

"I want to see her too." Monique said.

"No!" Treasure yelled.

Everyone looked at her in a very surprised manor. They thought she was upset but to refuse the family the rights to see her? It didn't make sense. Dr. Nyugen knew why because; Keysha was not dead.

"And why not?" Jackie asked.

"Yes, Treasure why I can't see my cousin who was more like my sister?! I want to say goodbye." Monique looked at her.

"It's my mother and I am in control of what happens to her."

"I understand that and we are here to help you through this Treasure." Jackie explained to her.

"What's really going on Treasure?" Monique started to get suspicious.

"She wouldn't want you to see her like that." Treasure said.

"I don't give a damn what she looks like." Monique shouted.

"I said no!" Treasure yelled.

"I know you must have lost your damn mind yelling at me." Monique walked towards her.

Dr. Nyugen could see there was about to be a family confrontation and he wanted to diffuse the situation. He definitely didn't want anyone from his staff to come in here and say that Keysha was not really dead.

Especially if he didn't know what she had in place for her mother.

"Treasure, can I please talk to you?" He asked

"Yes." She answered.

She stepped out into the hall with him. She knew he was going to ask her why she is doing this. Treasure knew it was time to put her plan of saving her mother into action and the doctor was going to be the one to do it for her. If not, her mother will be the last patient he would see, because she was going to go for his medical license.

"What the hell is wrong with Treasure?" Monique asked.

"Come on Monique, she just lost her mother and she has no father or grandmother just us." Jackie spoke.

"But mom really though, like cut the bullshit and let us help you." She said.

"Where is all this cussing coming from?" She asked.

"I guess I am channeling my inner Keysha." She laughed.

"I'm with you mommy, something's up." Harmony chimed in.

"Look, we will support her in anyway. Whatever she decides we will agree because we are all she has." Jackie explained.

"Agreed," Monique said.

"Agreed," Harmony also said.

Dr. Nyugen comes back into the room. To everyone's surprise Treasure is not with him. He had a very weird look on his face.

"Where's my niece?" Monique asked.

"She said she needed sometime to herself." He explained

"What? What the hell?" Monique looked at her mom.

"Remember what we just agreed to." Jackie said to her.

"Well, I know she would want me to be with her. Could you take me to her?" Harmony asked.

"She specifically said she didn't want to see anyone and would meet you guys at the house later."

"Okay, can we at least see my cousin Keysha." Monique asked.

"I'm sorry she said no one can see her. I have to honor what she says. She is the next to kin and makes all decisions." He said.

"I am about to show my ass in this hospital." Monique said.

"No, you are not. Let's go." Jackie said.

"No mom!" She said

"Mom, it's what she wants. Let's give her some space and see what tomorrow brings." Harmony begged.

"Ok but I'm not done with her, I want to see my cousin." Monique spoke.

"Once again, I am so sorry for your loss, and I will make sure Treasure gets home safely." Dr Nyugen expressed.

"Thank you so very much. "Jackie told him.

As soon as the family left, he hurried out of the room to find Treasure. He felt he could not do what she had asked of him. He stood at the elevator doors, sweating and talking to himself.

"Dr. Nyugen are you okay?" the nurse asked him.

"Oh yes, I didn't hear you." He replied.

"Well we need you, we have a shooting victim in route, eta is 2 minutes." She explained.

"What? I can't, I have to…" He started to say.

"Dr. Nyugen are you okay? You look a little flushed." She asked him.

"I'm okay, it has truly been a crazy day." He sighed.

Just at that moment, the ambulance pulled up and they were bringing out the patient flying past him. He knew that Treasure would have to wait and he had to attend to this patient.

"Let's go save lives." He smiled.

"Let's go." She smiled back.

Treasure took a deep breath as she stood outside the ICU door of her mother. She pushed the door open and immediately put her hand over her heart. All the monitors, tubes and smell of blood made her nauseous. It's not like she has never experience this scene before, it just really hit home. She walked towards her mother. Keysha was laying there looking as if she was dead already. Just as Treasure was about to touch Keysha's hand a nurse walked in.

"Hi can I help you?" She said.

"I was just coming to check on this patient, I was working in the ER when she came in. How is she?" Treasure asked.

The skinny white nurse with beautiful brown and blonde umbre' hairstyle was very kind and soft spoken. She walked up to Treasure and put her hands on her shoulder.

"If we only had more people that cared like you," she began to say.

"She is really hurt. The next couple of hours are really important for her survival." She explained.

Treasure tried to fight back the tears, but couldn't. She thought how hard her mother had it and she wished she could turn back the hands of time.

"Are you okay?" The nurse asked her.

"Yes, I'm sorry." Treasure spoke.

"Okay, I'm just going to check on her."

The nurse couldn't understand why Treasure was so emotional about a patient she had no relationship with. The nurse walked over to Keysha and looked her over. She took Keysha's blood pressure and she opened her eyes. Treasure was so happy to see her mother responding.

"How are you?" the nursed asked Keysha.

"I'm in so much pain, could you give me something please." Keysha asked.

"Of course you can, you've been through a lot today." She explained.

"Am I going to die?" Keysha asked her.

"Well, you have suffered some extensive wounds, but between me and you, you are a tough chick." She laughed.

"That I am, I have someone to live for." She smiled.

"Well whoever they are you really must love them, because you are doing great." She rubbed her hand.

"Yes, Ma'am it's my daughter, I need her right now." She wiped away tears.

"We going to pray that it comes to past, but you do have a visitor. One of our Nursing techs who was with you when you came in earlier. I'm going to get your pain medicine." She smiled at her.

The nurse hugged Treasure on her way out. Keysha motioned for Treasure to come closer. She couldn't really see that well she had two black eyes.

"Well hello there." Keysha said.

"Hello, how are you feeling?" Treasure asked

"I've been better but I'm here. Come closer I can't see you." Keysha said.

Treasure walked to the bed and Keysha reached for her hand. She was just happy to have an emotional contact with someone that was not out to judge her. She tried to squint to see Treasure clearly but could not. Treasure rubbed her head.

"I'm sorry I can't see very well, but I want to thank you for coming to check on me." She said.

"There is no other place I would rather be." Treasure said.

"You must really love your job, to visit a HIV convict." Keysha told her.

Treasure took her hand and kissed it. Keysha was a little taken back by this. Who was this girl? Should she be afraid?

"Mom" Treasure spoke.

"Mom?" Keysha asked confusedly.

"It's me mommy, I'm here for you." Treasure began to cry.

Keysha could not believe it; her baby was here with her. She didn't understand why GOD was blessing her at this moment. She pulled her to her and began hugging her. Even though she was in excruciating pain she didn't care.

"How Treasure? You work here?" She asked.

"Mom we don't have much time." Treasure said.

"Okay." Keysha listened.

"Don't tell anyone I'm your daughter." Treasure instructed.

Keysha felt horrible. She was thinking Treasure doesn't even want people to know she's my daughter. She couldn't blame her; she would be ashamed of herself too.

"Mom, Mom" Treasure spoke.

"Okay Treasure I won't tell anyone you are my daughter." She looked sad.

"Mom it's not what you think." Treasure tried to explain.

"I am an embarrassment to you baby." Keysha said.

"No mom that's not it. I love everything about you." Treasure kissed her forehead.

"Then what is it?" She asked.

"I'm getting you out of here, I have the perfect plan." She was getting excited.

"Treasure I don't want you to get caught up in my bullshit and go to jail." She told her.

"Mom I got this, remember who my mother is." She laughed

"Are you sure?" Keysha asked her.

"Mom yes trust me." She said.

"Till the day, I die." She laughed

"And it's not today!" She hugged her

"Oww Treasure." She screamed.

"Sorry mom." Treasure said.

Just then the nurse walked in and put the medication in her IV bag.

"Ok Miss Keysha you should be feeling better in minutes." She said.

"Thank you so much." Keysha said.

"Okay lady you are going to have to say your goodbyes now, she needs her rest."

She walked out of the room. Treasure grabbed her hand and kissed her mother.

"I got you babe." Treasure said.

Keysha was beginning to feel sleepy. She wasn't sure if she was dreaming, dead or if it was really true.

"I love you." Keysha said

"I love you more." Treasure whispered in her ears.

She turned to leave and Dr. Nyugen was standing in the doorway. He looked scared and concerned.

"How is she?" He asked

"She is doing very well." Treasure said.

"Treasure I can't do this." He said

"Oh really?" She said

Treasure reached in her scrub pockets and pulled out her phone and he wasn't quite sure what she was doing.

"Really Treasure I can't. Can you get off your damn phone?" He said.

Just then he got a message alert on his personal phone. He ignored it. He just wanted to not be involved with anything that would jeopardize his medical license.

"Aren't you going to check your message?" She asked

"No, I don't care about no message. For real Treasure we are done here. Your mom is going back to jail when she heals and there is nothing that we can do it about it." He explained.

"You think so, huh?" She smiled at him.

"Yes, it's the truth. I don't know what she did to go to jail, but it's not my business." He said.

"Well it became your business the first night you fucked me in that patient's room." She said.

"I'm done with this and I'm done with your ass." He grabbed her by her collar.

"First of all take your mutherfucking hands of me, before I be forced to fuck you up!"

He was a little intimidated but he knew he had the upper hand; she was a lowly tech, who would believe her anyways?

"Look at the fuckin message I sent you." She said.

"You sent me?" He looked surprised.

He looked at the message and started to look faint. He could not believe it. Treasure had sent him several videos of them having sex in the hospital.

"Why would you do this?" He asked.

"Didn't I tell you I needed your help? It wasn't a thoughtless request." She looked at him.

"Really?" He leaned up against the wall.

"So here's what's going to happen. Get my mother out here tonight, she better be in the same condition, I'm leaving her in." She told him.

"And how am I supposed to do that?" He asked.

"I don't give a fuck how you do it. You just better get it done and not leave a trace that she may be gone." She told him.

"I need time to figure it out." He pleaded.

"That's something you don't have. My mother better be at the place I told you to put her at. If not first thing in the morning and I do mean first thing, I will go the hospital's board of directors and the news about how Dr. Nyugen loves to have enema bags stuck up his ass to fucking cum." She stared at him.

"I understand." He said

"I truly hope you do. Now get the fuck out, you have work to do.

2 THE DESTRUCTION OF TWO SISTERS

Monique is sitting in her truck outside of her mother's house. She has really mixed feelings about what happened last night in the hospital. She was hoping her mom could help her calm down and come to some decision about Treasure and why she wouldn't let her see Keysha. She took a deep breath and stepped out unto the hot summer morning. She really needed her mom right now.

She walked up to the long brick rancher and noticed her step dad Xavier rocking back and forth in his chair. He looked really sad and she was wondering why, because he did not know Keysha. She walked over towards him.

"Hi Xavier." She said

"Hey Monique, how are you doing today?" He spoke.

"I have had better days." Monique said to him.

"Well your mom is having a really hard time." He told her.

"Yeah I know we all are; it's like our family is dwindling away."

"No your mom has been in the bed since you dropped her off yesterday. She has been crying and talking to herself." He told her.

"What?" Monique looked concerned because her mother was always very strong.

"She doesn't want me in there and keeps saying that her and Pam could have worked it out."

"Why didn't you call me?" She was beginning to get angry.

"I knew you was already going through a lot." He told her

"Nothing is more important than my mother. Nothing!" She told him.

Monique turned away and walked into the house. She started to feel uneasy, not knowing what she was going to find when she reached her mother's room. The home was so well kept; beautiful hardwood floors, perfectly placed furniture in the open concept family room and kitchen. Monique started down the hall towards her mom room. Her heart started beating faster and she was breathing hard. She reached the room and knocked on the door. There was no answer or an invitation to come in.

"Mom it's me can I come in please?" Monique has her head up against the door.

She got no response. So she twisted the knob and the door opened. She could not believe it. Her mom was lying in the bed knees to her chest crying. She ran over to her.

"Mom!" Monique yelled.

Jackie did not hear Monique. She was in bed thinking about how Pam life was. If she would have just told Monique and Keysha the truth, then maybe Keysha would have had a better life. If she wasn't so high and mighty, she could have made a difference. She could have forgiven Pam and just tried to love her more.

"Mom!" Monique yelled again

Monique wrapped her body around her mother and started squeezing her and kissing her.

"Come on mom, come on mommy!" She cried

"What's going on?" Xavier stood in the door way.

"Get out, I got this!" She yelled at him

At first Xavier stood there. All 6'4 of him. He was a chocolate man with a very in shape frame to be in his late fifties. He didn't budge. He was walking towards the both of them. He was a very gentle giant. He had never seen his wife like this, nor has his step daughter ever spoken to him like that.

"Stop right there Xavier." Jackie said.

Monique and Xavier both got silent and looked at Jackie. She seems to be coming around. He wanted to hug her and take her into his arms. So, he continued to walk up to the bed.

"I said stop right there Xavier!" She yelled again.

Monique was so terrified she let her mother go and slide down to the bottom of the bed. Xavier stopped and did not move. He felt upset that she would speak to him like that when all he wanted to do was love her.

"I need to speak to Monique alone." She said.

"I just want to make sure you're okay." He said.

"I'm okay baby I just have to speak with my daughter." She explained to him.

"Okay fine." He said

Jackie knew that she had hurt Xavier's feelings and would deal with him later. What she needed to talk to

Monique about is much more important right now. She took a deep breath and took Monique's hand.

"What is it mom?" She was so concerned

"I have to talk to you about your Aunt Pamela and Keysha."

"Is that what has you so upset?" She asked.

"Yes" She looked down at the ground.

"You can't tell me anything about Aunt Pam that would change the way I feel about her hateful ways."'" She said.

"It may change your mind." She touched her face.

"I doubt it, the way she had my cousin selling her ass for her thirsty ass greed for money." She told her.

"Monique shut the hell up!" She told her.

Monique was so shocked by her mother yelling and cussing at her, she didn't say a word.

"I need you to listen to what I have to tell you and hear the whole story"

"Ok, I'm listening.

3 THE LAYERS OF PAMELA

Pamela was the only child born to Mary and Charles Williams. Life with her parents had been pure hell. Mary was a homemaker and stood a stout five feet tall, with long black hair. Her father was six foot two with big shoulders and looked damn near white. As long as she could remember they fought about everything. Her father was a drunk and his whole check would go to the local bar. Every Friday her mother would try to have the house cleaned up for him. The family stayed in a two-bedroom box house. They had one couch in the living room and a T.V with aluminum foil wrapped on the antenna. In the kitchen, there was a table that leaned to one side and had to be propped up with anything to even out the other three legs. Mary did the best with her limited food supply so she had to get creative with her meals. Tonight it was fried bologna, rice and pork'n beans. The door opened and it was her dad. He reeked of liquor and she knew that it was over for her mom.

"Hi, Daddy."

"Hey, baby girl."

He put her down and walked over to the stove. The tension in the air was thick and her mother looked very nervous.

"What the fuck is this mess you cooked?"

"Charles, it is all we had. I am doing the best that I can." He slapped her.

"Don't do this, Charles. Not tonight."

"Don't do what?" He picked her up and threw her back down on the floor.

Pamela began to cry and scream. She did not want her dad to beat up her mother.

"Pam go in your room while Daddy talks to Mommy."

She walked to her room but never went in. She hid by the doorway and watched. Her dad walked towards her mother. She was pleading with him not to hit her.

"Charles, please don't hit me."

"Charles, please don't hit me," he mocked her.

"I do the best I can with the little bit of stamps I get. I can't get a job because Pam is only four years old and we can't afford a babysitter."

"Well, your best isn't good enough."

"Charles, if you would bring some of your

paycheck home we could have a little more than what we have now."

"Bitch, who the fuck do you think you are talking to? I don't do enough for this family?"

"I didn't mean…"

"Did I tell you to talk?"

Mary knew to shut up because she knew regardless, she was going to get her ass whipped tonight. She just wanted to make it as painless as possible.

"I can do what I want with my money, do you understand? Do you fucking understand me? Now your bitch-ass can talk."

"Yes, Charles."

"What?"

"Yes sir, Charles."

"Better. Now take off your clothes."

"For what?"

"You questioning me?"

"No sir."

She began to take her clothes off, not sure what he was going to do to her. She stood their butt-ass naked. She glimpsed over at the door and saw Pam hiding. She wanted to tell her to go in her room but was scared to. She was not allowed to speak.

"Now you want to tell Charles what to do, right?"

Charles began to take off his thick leather belt. He wrapped the strap around his hand with just the buckle hanging.

"Charles, please don't hit me!"

He reached his hand back and swung forward with all his might. He struck her and she fell and began to scream.

"Mary, get your ass up and put your hands on the chair and don't move! If you do, I am going to fuck you up for real!"

She got up, her back stinging from the first blow. Pamela's mom put both her hands on the chair and stood there.

"Do not speak or move or I will kill you!"

He continued to hit her and hit her. She stood there not moving, tears ran down her face. It seemed like forever that he beat her.

"You can move now."

She could barely move. She went to grab her clothes and put them on.

"Leave those clothes there; come and get on your knees and take care of me."

She knew that meant suck his dick until he came on her face. He loved to degrade her and keep her under his control.

"Charles, please. Pam…"

"Mary, my arms are not tired. Do you want some more? "Pam is in her room and she knows to stay there. You say one more word and I'm going to hurt you."

She walked over towards her husband and glanced over at her daughter. She did not want her to see this. As Charles pulled his pants down he noticed Pam. He smiled and told Mary to hurry up. She knelt down and began performing oral sex on him. Sickened at the fact that her daughter was watching, she threw up. He went into frenzy and began to punch and kick her.

"Oh! My dick ain't good enough for you to suck?"

"Charles, please! Pam is by the door."

"Pam, get in here!"

"Charles, no. Don't!"

Pam came in the kitchen. Her heart was pounding. She did not know what was going on but her dad was hurting her mommy.

"Since you want to see what big people do, sit your ass over in that chair over there."

Her dad had never talked to her in that tone before. She was terrified.

"Mary, lay your ass on the table and open up your legs."

"Pam, go in your room."

"I told her to sit her ass right there. Now get your ass on the table like I said."

"Charles, in front of your daughter?"

"Mary, get on the fucking table now! I want some pussy and yours belongs to me."

"I can't do that in front of her."

"I tell you what: Either you get up here or Pam

does."

Mary could not believe he would even contemplate raping his own daughter. She got on the table and laid back.

"Just what I thought. Pam, what I am about to do is what all women do for their man, and one day you will have to do it for you husband. If you get one, don't be a dumb bitch like your mom."

He opened her legs and she began to shake with fear. He took his fingers and stuck them inside her.

"Damn, your pussy is dry and tired. You need to get that bitch wet because I am not trying to burn myself fucking you."

He got up and went to the cabinet and got the cooking oil. He opened her legs and poured it all over her.

"Yeah, because Daddy likes a juicy pussy."

He pulled her to the end of the table and turned her on her stomach. He put his dick inside her and began moving back and forth. Pam just looked at her dad. Not knowing what he was doing, she began to cry.

"Pam, baby, it is going to be alright."

"Go to your room and stay there this time!"

She got off the chair and ran to her room, not to return to hide outside the door again. She could hear her dad screaming and she didn't know why. She shut her door and went to bed. Mary came in the room to check on her daughter, who was already asleep.

"I promise, baby, it will get better," she whispered to her.

The next day would be the last day she would see her father. He said he was going to the bar and he never came back. She overheard her mom on the phone talking to one of her friends, saying he could not forgive himself for how he made Pamela watch, and she would be better off without him.

4 PAMELA CHANGES FOREVER

It had been two years since Pam had seen her dad. Mary was dating a man name Kevin Jones and he wanted to marry her. She would never marry again and just planned to live together. Kevin was a little taller than Mary and had gorgeous honey brown skin and a beautiful attitude. She met him while she attended college. He was a professor there and encouraged her to pursue her dream of becoming a social worker to help other battered women. He was also very kind to Pamela. He took the whole family out, not just Mary. She made it very clear that she was a package deal.

"Pamela, come her."

Mary and Kevin were sitting on the new patio furniture they had just gotten to go with the swing-set in the backyard. Mary looked so happy she was glowing.

"Yes Mom?"

"I know that you are only five but I need to tell you something."

She didn't know what they wanted to tell her but she could tell it was serious. Her mom and Mr. Kevin were holding hands.

"I'm a big girl."

"We know."

"Well, Mommy and Mr. Kevin are going to have a baby."

Pam just looked at them. She really did not know what it meant but she knew she would have somebody to play with.

"Yeah! I'm going to have a little sister!"

"Well, we don't know if it is a girl or boy yet. Are you okay with this?"

"Yes, now I have someone to play with." She skipped back to her swing-set.

"That went well."

"Yes, it did."

Later that year Jackie was born and everything seemed to be going very well with the family. Pamela did everything for her sister. She liked pretending to be the mommy.

Several years passed by and Pam was a teenager and Jackie a pre-teen and the troubles began.

She began to realize that her parents treated Jackie better than her. Pam wanted a car because she had just turned sixteen. She had just come out of the DMV.

"So, Mom, when can I get a new car?"

"Pam, as soon as you save half the money, Kevin and I will pay the other half."

"Good thing for me! All that working this summer paid off and I have fifteen hundred saved up."

"Okay, Pam, let's talk to your dad when we get home."

On the way home she could only think about what kind of car she would get. Pam had worked all summer at McDonald's. She saved all her checks, not even spending one dime. She wanted to go to school this year in a nice ride. They pulled up in to the driveway of the bi-level house. The lawn was landscaped with flowers everywhere. As they parked her sister and dad were in the swing on the porch smiling. Jackie ran up to the car.

"Did you get your L's?"

"And you know this, man!"

"Yeah girl, I can go to the mall all the time now."

"We."

"Yeah, we, right."

Pam got out of the big black shiny SUV and walked over to the porch where her mom and dad were swinging.

"Dad, I got them."

"That's great, baby girl."

"So when can we go car shopping? I want to begin school in style."

"You have money for a car?"

"Yes, I have fifteen hundred saved up." She was so proud of herself.

"You still have to buy clothes for school and you have to get your school supplies."

She could not believe this! He was going back on his word. Her mother just looked at him but did not question him.

"You said if I saved my money for half you guys would pay the other half."

"Did we? I don't remember."

"Mom remembers."

"Pam just don't worry about it. You will get your car, just keep saving."

She could not believe her mom would take up for him like that. They both said it and now she had to get all her stuff by herself.

"So you are just going to take up for him even though he is lying?"

Kevin jumped up and slapped her dead in the face. Her mom sat there and looked at the floor. Jackie leapt on his back.

"Get off my sister!"

He turned around and put her in a bear hug.

"Baby, stop! Don't hit your father."

"Why are you hitting my sister?"

"Your sister is disrespectful towards me and I am not going to take it. Your mother and I pay the bills here, not you. You will do what I say. I'm saying right now, apologize to me."

Pam stared at that fool like he was crazy. She'd be damned if she apologized to him.

"Apologize for what? It is true. You are a liar."

He tries to slapped her again and her mother finally got in the way.

"Kevin, what are you doing?"

"She is not going to talk to me like that. Hell, she is not even my daughter but I take care of her like she is mine. She will not disrespect me!"

"Well you took on that responsibility when you got involved with me."

"I have one daughter and that is the only one I will be taking care of. If she wants anything she should ask her trifling-ass father."

"I will, you bastard."

Why did she say that? That was the straw that broke the camel's back.

"That's it! When I come back, I want her gone."

"What are you talking about?"

"Mary, I can't take her anymore. It is either her

or me."

He jumped in his car and pulled off. Kevin was gone about a week when he called her mother on the phone.

"Hello."

"Hi, baby. I miss you."

"I miss you, too. When are you coming home?"

"Did you contact Pam's father?"

Her mom took the receiver from her ear and looked at it.

"Are you serious? You won't come back unless she is gone?"

"I meant what I said. I won't deal with her. I will take Jackie and we can get a place together. You and Pam can get a place."

"I can't believe you want me to choose between my daughter and you."

"Mary, I love you, but I can't do it anymore."

Mary realized he was not playing and her desire to have a family would win out over her motherly responsibility to her child.

"I will get everything ready."

"Okay, baby, I will be over to get Jackie."

Pamela was hiding behind the door and began to cry. She knew she would be leaving the only family she had ever known to stay with a man she barely knew.

****

5 A BLESSING OR A CURSE

Pamela could not believe it. Kevin was dead, he had a heart attack. She had to admit the smile on her face was the satisfaction of knowing he was dead. She could be a family with her mom and sister again. She could finally leave Lil Sal, who was her sugar daddy. He was 5'4, tanned skin, a head full of products and always wearing a muscle shirt. If you haven't figured it out Lil Sal was Italian. Something she was definitely not into. He was the right hand trigger man for his father the head of a mob family here in Chicago. She met him when she was twenty years old. Pamela saved his life and he in return saved hers. Pamela began to think about that day.

"Pamela, get your ass up." James yelled.

"Dad I'm tired." Pamela whined.

"Don't call me dad." He lowered his head.

"Ok, whatever."

"Look, Donald is coming over; we need to get our story straight about his money."

"What money? I have nothing to do with that."

James reached over and slapped Pamela off the bed, blood began to trickle out of her nose. She refused to cry as she couldn't bring herself to display that weakness to her father. She looked around at the dirty studio apartment. Dirty dishes everywhere, heroin needles on the table, beer bottles on the floor. It was so nasty, and her mother sent her here to live like this.

"Get your ass up and make yourself presentable, you may have to suck a dick or something." He said.

"I just had an abortion I can't have sex right now." She pleaded.

"Look, your mouth is just fine. Get yourself together like I said." Looking dead in her eyes.

Pamela goes to the bathroom to clean the warm running blood from her face. The bathroom was just as nasty as the rest of the house. There was mold and a black ring around the tub. Toothpaste on the sink, dirty clothes on the floor and empty toilet tissue rolls all over the floor, there was also McDonald's napkins on the back of the toilet seat, Pamela stole those because there was never any tissue in the house. Pamela opened the closet hoping there was a clean washcloth in there to clean her face. While grabbing for it, she accidently knocks over a towel, she goes to put it back and a gun falls out.

"Pamela hurry the fuck up, there here." James sounded nervous.

She took a deep breath and prayed to herself that it would not be her last. Taking one last look at in the mirror to make sure she was as cute as possible, she never knew if she would have to beg for her life or not. Pamela opens the door and walks out. There stood three guys, she smiled at them and they never smiled back. The first guy was very tan, rippling with muscles and obviously a lot of product in his hair. Next to him was a plain looking white man in a grey business suit with a green tie, carrying a brief case and wearing black rimmed glasses. To the right of him was a short stout and also very tan Italian guy, dressed in a very tight tee shirt and leather jacket and black jeans. I came out and sat on the chair making sure not to speak unless spoken to. Talking out of turn could get you killed.

"What's good Tony?" My dad said.

"Cut the fucking pleasantries." Tony said in a very thick Jersey sounding accent.

Tony was the very big Italian guy who stood at least 6'6. He stepped towards my dad.

"Look you jungle monkey, where is Big Larry's money." He grabbed James by his neck.

"Tony I don't have it but if you give me a couple more weeks, I promise…"

Both the Italian guys start to kick and beat him, the white guy just sat there and watch. I secretly love watching him so weak and getting his ass kicked. Next thing you know the white guy opens his brief case and pulls out a small stack of papers.

"James my paperwork shows me that you owe $26,000, how do you plan on making this payment today?"

"Really Donald? Look around at my place; I don't have $26,000 to my name."

Wrong answer the two muscle guys said. They began beating him again.

"Please stop you're going to kill him." Pamela pretended to care.

They continued to beat and kick him. So Pamela threw herself on top of him, thinking it would stop the beatings. They began to beat her and one of them picked her up and slung her onto the sofa. The back of her neck was throbbing. Big Tony picked her dad up by the neck and began to choke him. Next thing was a gun shot and everyone stopped in their tracks.

"Oh shit this crazy bitch has a gun!" Big Tony screamed.

James pushed big Tony back off of him and he started to grasp for air. Everyone was silent. Pamela's heart was beating in her ears and she could barely here anything that was being said. Donald started to move closer to Pamela with his hands up but very slowly.

"You don't want to do this sweetie, these are some really bad guy's right here and the boss won't hesitate at hunting you down and killing you." He pleaded.

She pointed the gun at him and he froze. She didn't know what to do, should she pull the trigger or hand the gun over. Pamela knew either way she was dead, on the run for the rest of her life or her life ending right here in this living room.

"Fuck them boo, shoot every last one of these mutherfuckers. Let them know they can't fuck with us."

He began to pace back and forth rubbing his head. He walked past the short Italian guy and punched him in the face. He fell to the ground and began to spit out blood.

"Yeah bitch you're not so tough now, huh."

Big Tony started to reach around his back.

"Don't do it mutherfucker, don't do it." Pamela yelled. James walked over to him and searched him and grabbed the gun.

"You had a gun nigga; you ain't killing anybody today bitch." James yelled. "This is my gun now, so you beg for your life bitch! Big steroid looking ass bitch!

He walked around Tony, hitting him with the gun.

Tony was scared.

"James please." He begged

James walked around one more time then shot him in the head. Big Tony was lying in a pool of blood. The smaller guy jumped back and was very scared feeling like he would be next.

"I'm the king of this bitch and little Italy your ass is next." James pointed the gun.

James was acting crazier than usual. He sat down and shot up his heroin and began to nod out.

"I'm going to kill the both of you. Then I'm going to take my whore of a daughter to California and sell her until I can't get one damn cent for her. Trick ass whore." He laughed.

"This is how you talk about your daughter, who just saved your life?" Donald said.

"Fuck her; she ain't my real daughter anyway. Her whore ass mother was already pregnant when I met her. I just felt sorry for the whore, so I married her to make her a proper woman.

Pamela was crushed. This man isn't even her father and he had been pimping her out. James put her onto drugs and beat her daily. Pamela has had four abortions and not even knowing who the fathers were. Her mother knew this and still she sent her to live with this monster.

"I have nothing to do with that but this guy right here is little Sal and if his father finds out that you killed him, the pain he will inflict on the both of you is beyond anything you could imagine." Donald said.

"Fuck big Sal! Ya'll came for me, now I'm gunning for you." James waved the gun around.

By now lil Sal realizes he is going to die and sticks his chest out and plans on going out like a big man.

"You a big man huh." James walks up to him and puts the gun to his head.

"It's the life I live, nigger." Lil Sal says.

"Please don't do this!" Donald yells.

Lil Sal closes his eyes and sweat runs down his forehead. There is a loud bang, followed by silence and Lil Sal opens his eyes. James is lying on the floor with a whole in his head and Pamela standing over him. Donald and Lil Sal both breathed a sigh of relief.

"Thank you so much, thank you." Lil Sal hugged her.

"I know that was hard for you." Donald kissed her hand.

"It wasn't hard at all, you heard him I wasn't his fucking daughter." Pam stared.

Donald took the gun out of Pamela's hand and walks over to Lil Sal. They are talking and rubbing their heads. They both look down at Big Tony and look back at Pamela. She knew that she was a loose end and more than likely would be next to have a bullet in her head.

"Hey what about her, your dad is going to want her dead too." Donald said.

"True but if he found out that she saved my life he will be indebted to her." Lil Sal explained.

"So what are we going to do with her? We are still talking about $26,000 that is not going away." Donald looking puzzled.

"I will pay it and take her with me." Lil Sal Said.

"What!"

"She saved me." He smiled.

Oh my god they're walking over towards me. Pamela just knew she was gone. She didn't know if she should run or scream. She decided death might be less painful than being a live living like this.

"What's your name?" Sal asked.

"Pamela, why?"

"Today is your lucky day." He smiled.

"Don't you mean your lucky day; I just killed the only person I knew as my dad. I'm sure your dad doesn't want me around. So I'm next right?" Pamela glared at him.

"Correction it's our lucky day. Thank you again for saving me and I would like to do the same for you. I want to put you in rehab and have you come stay with me no strings attached."

"No strings attached, no sex." Pamela said.

"Nothing unless we agree as adults."

Pamela chose to go with Lil Sal. She put her hands out to seal the deal. He hugged her and kissed her hand.

"Let's go Donald nothing else left here." Sal said.

Lil Sal, Donald and Pamela left the apartment with the bodies in there and closed the door and never looked back.

6 A FAMILY REUNION

Lil Sal pulls up to the O'Hare International Airport. Pamela was so nervous. Could it be? Is she truly finished with the mob and that lifestyle? She secretly would miss Sal. Even though he has a wife and two kids, he still treated her like she was number one. He put her up in a waterfront condo, got her off drugs taught her how to speak like a lady. Deep down she really loved him. Yet, she knew her place would always be second place to the wife and kids. She was black and Italian no-no, so she would always be behind the scene and a secret.

"Are you sure you want to do this?" Lil Sal asked.

"Yes, Sal this is all the family I have left in the world." She caressed his face.

"I love you and I don't want you to go." He pleaded.

"We could never be together. I'm black and you're married with kids. Your father will never go for that.

And personally I don't want to break up any families."
She smiled.

He got out of the car and went to the trunk. Lil Sal
pulled out her luggage. He opened the back door and
pulled out the fur coat. Pamela reached for her door and
he quickly grabbed it.

"Here put this on." Sal told her.

"I don't need this, it really doesn't get that cold in
Georgia."

"Take it, please."

"No Sal, I need to make a clean break, from Chicago
and you."

"I won't let you go." He hugged her.

"But I have already let you go. Go to Gina and be a
wonderful, faithful husband and father. We are done."
She kissed him

Pamela picked up her luggage and walked in the airport
and never looked back. Once inside the airport it was
super crowded and she was looking for Southwest
Airlines. She took a deep breath and headed to retrieve
her first-class ticket and head to Savannah Georgia.

Pamela was beginning to have second thoughts should she go back to Sal and those comforts, but how long would that last. They were beginning to board and she got on the plane, terrified of the uncertainty that lay ahead.

****

"Everyone please buckle your seat belts and return to the upright position and prepare for landing." The flight attendant announced.

Jackie and Mary stood at the arrival terminal waiting for Pamela. They were both nervous. The last time they saw Pamela it was when Mary sent her away to go stay with her father. She never forgave Mary for that. Jackie just prayed it would be a happy reunion and that Pamela would stay in Georgia and be a part of her life again. Mary was just hoping Pamela would still love her and allow her to apologize for all the wrong doings. There was a steady stream of people coming and there was no site of Pamela yet. Jackie was afraid she had not come. Then all of a sudden Pamela appeared. There she was, a beautiful black woman with skin tight jeans, black knee high boots, a beautiful pea coat and long black wavy hair, not hers but you couldn't tell unless you knew her. Jackie ran up to her.

"Pam." She hugged her.

"Oh my, knock me over." Pamela smiled.

"Girl I missed you so much." Jackie jumped up and down.

"You missed me, really?" Looking surprised.

"Of course I missed you, you're my big sis." Jackie said.

"Okay." Pamela feeling uncomfortable.

"You have a lot of luggage."

"Not too much, I hope that's okay." Pamela said.

"Girl of course not." Jackie smiled.

While Jackie and Pamela waited on the luggage to come down the ramp, Pamela saw a lot of families hugging and kissing. She felt jealous. Is this family reunion going to really work? Then she hears a familiar voice.

"Hello Pamela."

She turns around. "Mother." Pamela replies.

Mary gets closer to Pamela and gives her a hug.
Pamela just stands there and doesn't know if she should
hug her or slap the shit out of her. She feels nothing for
this woman but hate. She was so happy her sister
interrupts them. Mary pulls away and wipes away tears.

"My two most favorite people in the world, besides my
husband Gerald." Jackie smirks at Pamela.

"Well somebody is getting some real good dick."
Pamela said.

"Pamela not in front of mommy." Jackie looking
embarrassed.

"Oh I'm sure she doesn't mind; how do you think we
got her? Right Mommy." Pamela rolled her eyes.

"Yes baby, we are all grown here." Mary said.

"Oh, here are my bags." Pamela realized.

"Great let's get them and go meet my hubby." Jackie
smiled.

"Well let's go meet the hubby then." She hugged
Jackie.

They all grabbed the luggage and rolled it out of the airport. Jackie's husband was arguing with a police officer about being parked in front of the airport and was about to give him a ticket. Jackie, Pamela and Mary runs to the truck.

"Come on officer really." Gerald said. "I'm just here to pick up my sister-in-law."

"Sir I don't care who you came to pick up, you can't just park here."

"Excuse me officer, please re-consider giving my brother in law a ticket please. I'm sure we can work something out." Pamela winked.

"Ma'am I don't think so." The officer replied.

"Really sir, really." Jackie asked.

Look you people are getting on my nerves, when he looks up from Gerald's license and gets speechless when he sees Pamela.

"Oh hello. Are you the sister in law?" He questions her.

"Why yes, I am." Pamela smiles.

"Yes, this is my sis." Gerald smiles.

He gets out the truck and grabs the suitcases and places them in the trunk. Mary and Jackie get in the truck and buckle up. Pamela and the officer step away from the truck to have a private conversation. Gerald walks over to make sure everything is okay. He also needs his driver license back.

"Is everything okay officer." Gerald asked

"Yeah everything is great." "Oh here is your license, we good."

"I will call you tonight Xavier, if that's okay."

"That will be fine Pamela, see you later hopefully."

"Oh you can bet on that."

Gerald and Pamela walk back and jump into the truck. Both with goofy smiles on their faces, Gerald was so happy because he got out of a ticket; and with him being in the military, he didn't need any trouble. Pamela was happy because she was going to get some black dick tonight, finally. She must admit, Lil Sal had a big dick, but there's nothing like black Mandingo. Let's hope its Mandingo and not tiny tot dick.

"Yes sis, that's what I'm talking about," Gerald high fived Pamela.

"I got you bro, that's what family is about. Helping each other out."

"What happened?" Jackie looking puzzled.

"Your sister made sure I didn't get a ticket."

"Good, thanks Pamela."

"Girl no problem."

"Well how did you do that?" Mary asked.

"I told him I would go out with him." Pamela responded.

"Well you need to be careful, Pam. You don't know anything about these people."

"Well Mary, I think I will be just fine. I have been taking care of myself since you sent me to go live with my father."

Mary shut up and swallowed hard. She wanted to cry but did not because she knew she deserved the anger that was directed towards her. The tension was so thick you could cut it with a knife. They road in silence for the next twenty minutes. Once they pulled up to the beautiful brick home. Gerald broke the silence with a joke.

"Okay Pam, what other trouble can you get me out of?"

"Anything for my brother." She rubbed his back.

He felt uncomfortable and grabbed her stuff and took it into the house. She walked in and her sister's home was beautiful. It felt so loving. The living room was the first room you enter. It was a grey oversized sectional with beautiful yellow and white flowered pillows. Soft butter colored curtains. She felt so jealous inside; she craved unconditional love like her sister was receiving from her husband. He was brushing her hair out of her face, caressing her shoulders and kissing her neck. Pamela then notices a family portrait; she really wanted to destroy it.

"Hey sis, come on. I will show you to your room."

"Sounds good to me, I could really use a shower and to get ready for my date."

"You're really going out with a stranger you just met." Mary said.

"That's how strangers become friends, they go out."
Pamela said sarcastically.

"Jackie I can't, I'm going home."

"Mom, don't leave please."

"No Jackie, please let her go." Pam raised her voice.

"She is never going to forgive me."

"Please we just buried my dad three days ago, I can't with you guys." Jackie began to cry.

"What is there to forgive? You sent me to a man who beat the hell out of you and then beat the hell out of me." Pamela screamed.

Gerald came running from the back of the house. He didn't know what was going on. Pamela was yelling at Mary. Jackie was up against the wall holding her face crying.

"What the hell is going on here, baby calm down!!" Gerald screamed.

"It's just a lot of family crap that needs to be resolved." Jackie spoke.

"I'm leaving Gerald; I did not mean to disrespect your home." Mary said to him.

"I'm only going to say this once, respect my house and my mutherfucking wife. My house is always a calm place. I don't know what is going on with the two of you but leave my wife out of it." He explained.

"I wasn't trying to start anything." Pamela tried to explain.

"Look Pamela, I really don't know you and I really don't care to know you after this bullshit." "Don't start shit in my house or your ass is back to Chicago."

"Gerald please that's my sister."

"Baby I don't give a fuck."

"I'm good sis." She kissed her on the cheek.

"Pam, I don't know you and you don't know me. One thing you should know is I don't play and I mean what the fuck I say." He walked away.

Mary walked out the door. Jackie showed Pamela to her room. Pamela laid on the bed in disbelief. She just got there and her and Mary already had their first fight.

****

Pamela awakes from her nap refreshed and renewed. All she could think about was her possible date. She pulled a piece of paper with the name William McKinley and his phone number. Pamela was in the motion of reaching for the phone when the aroma of soul food was coming in the room and then there was a knock at the door.

"Yes." Pamela answered.

"Hey your finally up, I cooked are you hungry?" Jackie smiled.

"Girl yes, it smells heavenly. What did you cook?"

"Oh just some collard greens, macaroni and cheese, cornbread and peach cobbler." Jackie grinned.

"You act like that was something slight. Well did you put your foot in it?"

"Both feet girl." They both laughed.

"Well let me make a quick call and I will be right out there to get it in."

"Make your call and come join us." She winked at her. Pamela got up from the bed and started to rehearse what she would say to William. Should she be sexy or a bubbly blond. Then she realized that she was doing all this and no one could even see her and she began to laugh. Pam grabs the phone and then makes the number. She clears her throat.

"Hello." The husky voice said.

"Well hello yourself, sexy officer." Trying to sound sexy.

"I've been waiting on your call all day, I thought you forgot about me."

"Never that. I had to take a shower and a nap. You know spend time with the family."

"So what's your plan after family time?"

"I thought being with you tonight and maybe early morning breakfast as well."

"Sounds good! Where and what time?" William eagerly asks.

Pamela gave him the address and they agreed to meet up at 9:00. Once she was off the phone she began to dance around the room.

"Yes, guess who is getting some dick tonight. Me that's who." She was singing.

She opens the room door and made her way to the kitchen where Jackie set the table and had the food out on the table. The aroma was intoxicating. She could not imagine how beautiful the table was. It was a black six seating dinner table, plate settings; the food was in beautiful dishes made for the food that was prepared. She sat down with Jackie and Gerald to enjoy a family meal, which she hasn't had sense leaving her mom and sister to live with her father.

"This is beautiful Jackie."

"I'm glad you like it sis, this is all for you."

"Well hello Gerald, I hope you're not still mad at me." Pamela looked at him.

"Well Pam, I am still pissed but you ladies need to work out your issues, as long as you don't hurt my babe."

"Enough table talk let's eat." Jackie smiled.

"Yes cuz I have a date." Pamela giggled.

"The Police Officer?" Jackie inquired.

"Yes, we are going to Two Guys."

"I don't know if you will like it. It's like a little whole in the wall. It's not Chicago."

"I don't care, we just spending a little time together."

"The extra set of keys are on the table by the door, use it." Gerald smiled.

Dinner was done and great. Pamela helps Jackie clear the dishes and clean the kitchen. It is obvious that Jackie is a housewife to a letter T. Gerald definitely ran the home. Jackie loves catering to her husband. Pamela thought if she had a man like that she would stay home and please him all day too.

****

Pamela can't believe it is 7 o'clock in the morning and she is just getting dropped off from the most boring sex with William. William had picked Pamela up in a candy red mustang with leather interior seats. He was dressed to impress in his black suit and dress shoes. He smelled so good, just had Pamela's mouth was watering. Pamela was just as fly. A little black dress is always the best and a pair of shiny black stiletto's. A beaded clutch purse and simple accessories.

"Let me get that door for you." William said.

"You look and smell delicious."

He walked around to the other side of the door. Pamela sat back and buckled up. William just stared at her. She looked gorgeous and his dick was getting hard just looking at her.

"Is something wrong? Why are you just staring at me?" Pamela looked perplexed.

"You look so sexy, I just want to lean over and kiss you."

"So what are you waiting for, lean your ass over here and get this sweetness."

He leaned in to kiss her, Pamela's lips were so soft. He rubbed on her thighs and he began to moan. Pamela could tell that he was getting really excited. She had to stop him and save it for later. She really wanted to get her dance on and end the night with sex.

"Okay, okay save some for later."

"So there is going to be a later?"

"If you act right and I have a good time, will you."

William pulls off and heads to the club. While riding in the car William is attempting to sing and he sounds horrible. Pamela looks out the window at the people as she passes them and thinks these people are country as hell. A couple more street lights and there is a line of half-dressed girls. The music was bumping from inside of the club. Flashing lights around the sign Two Guys. It was a little red neck looking place. William pulled in the parking lot and turned off the ignition.

"We are here."

"I see, but it is so small."

"It's not Chicago, but we will have fun."

Pamela walks in the club hand and hand with William. To her amazement it was really live in the club. The music was great and it was packed and everyone was dancing and having a good time. No drama in sight. A far cry from her Chicago days, somebody getting their ass shot or cut at a party was expected. William took her straight to the bar and ordered her a drink and found them a table. He pulled out Pamela's chair and she sat down. She was not use to someone treating her like a lady. He sat down and began to sip on his drink.

"You want to dance?"

"I would love to dance." She jumped up.

They got on the floor and she began to throw her hips left and right. William actually was a great dancer. He was hanging right with her. They danced for about twenty minutes straight. Pamela was getting tired when a slow song was being played. William pulled her close to him and began to move back and forth. She really loved being held so closely with someone of the opposite sex, hell anyone.

"Yo man the music stopped." A short dark-skinned guy with a gold tooth and greasy hair spoke.

They both just started laughing.

"Do you want to get out of here?" Pamela said.

"I sure do." William smiled.

Pamela left the club headed to William's house and sex was definitely on both of their minds. They pull up to a brick rancher very well taken care of from the outside. She couldn't wait to see the inside. This could be her new residence, if all goes well. William turned the key to the door and invited Pamela in. The house smelled wonderful and he turned the lights on. The house was gorgeous! We entered the house and were immediately standing in the living room. There was huge black leather sectional, with read accent pillows. There were hardwood floors throughout the rooms. Every wall had beautiful abstract artwork with accents of red everywhere and a red wall where a small piano sat.

"Do you play?" Pamela smiled.

"Actually I do."

"Play me a little something."

"Okay."

William sat at the piano and began to play. Pamela thought it would be just like the sounds that came out of his mouth in the car. To her surprise it was nothing like that. He played beautifully, she didn't know what it was but it was wonderful. She stood behind him and kissed his neck.

"What was that you played, I love it?"

"Stevie Wonder, Ribbon in the Sky."

He turned around and sat Pamela on his lap and began to kiss her. Pamela was feeling quite warm between her legs. He slid his hands up under her dress and looked at Pamela. She didn't have any panties on. Pamela looked at him and smiled. He put his fingers in her pussy that was already wet from the song. Pamela began to moan. He stood her up and turned her around and unzipped her dress, but made her leave the shoes on. William then lifted her up and places her on the piano.

"Get on all fours."

"I have no problem with that."

William was eating her pussy with such precision; she just knew the sex was going to be the shit. He tasted her for thirty minutes straight. Pamela's knees were so bruised up for kneeling on the piano for a half an hour. William finally stops and picks Pamela up and carries her to the room. She was so happy! She liked to get her pussy licked just like the next bitch, but damn.

The room was dark and cold. William laid her down on some cold sheets and reached in his drawer for a condom. He took off all his clothes and climbed on top of Pam. He was pumping and huffing. Pamela could not believe it this nigga had a small dick. This mutherfucker really think he is really getting it in. Pamela was so upset, all that pussy licking and no dick. This went on for twenty minutes the first time and thirty the second time. Pamela just laid there pissed off.

"Baby that was so good." William said.

"It was good to me too." She lied.

He turned over and went to sleep. Pamela was so pissed that she fell asleep as well.

****

Jackie peeked her head in the room. Pamela was still sleep. She decided to go back to bed and make love to her own husband. Jackie tip toed into her room. She stood just inside the door, when she decided to take her clothes off. The room was freezing from the fan blowing left and right. Jackie walked to Gerald's side of the bed and pull the comforter back. She slid her hand in the slit of his boxers and pulled his dick out and began to lick his head. He began to moan and grabbed Jackie's head pulling it back and forth.

"Good Morning. It's nothing like waking up to your man being saluted."

"Good Morning." She tried to mutter but had a mouth full of dick.

"Baby okay, okay. I can't take anymore.

He reached to get a condom, but Jackie pushed his hand away. He looked shocked. Yes, they were married but they always used condoms. They were married and were talking about having a baby. Jackie got up and sat on his dick and began to ride him. Gerald was trembling; he loved early morning sex, before a round of golf with his boys. Jackie was feeling it and was exploding all over her husband. He was beginning to feel out of control. He grabs Jackie's nipples that was hard from the fan blowing on them and this turned Gerald on as well as Jackie. He flips Jackie over and begins to go deep and she screams. That sound made Gerald go crazy and he began to fuck her even harder. Both sweating like they just had a full work out finally reaches their climax and relaxes. They look at each other and both laugh.

"What are you laughing at?" Gerald asks.

"You look so crazy when you cum."

"No crazier than you when I'm hitting that spot and your neck starts to tighten and jerk back. I thought you were having a seizure. Oh yeah seizing of this big dick!" Oh Rah!

"Does everything have to be military?"

"Sorry babe, let's get in the shower and get the day started."

There was a knock at the door. Pamela started to act as if she was still sleep, since she could hear Jackie screaming through the house. She may as well get up and start the day.

"Come in."

"Hey sis, how was your date?"

"I should have stayed home."

"Why?"

"Can you say the worst sex EVER?"

"Ever?"

"Ever, he had the smallest dick. Oh he could eat the pussy but that was a set up for that short coming. If you know what I mean."

"Girl I actually don't." Jackie smiled.

"I heard you, hell the whole neighborhood heard you."

"Well you know, what can I say?"

"Okay you a bad bitch now."

"Yeah I guess."

"I know that's right, handle your business. If I had a husband that treated me like yours, I would be fucking him all the time. Does he have a big dick?"

"Hell yeah. I love that dick too."

"Oww Oww."

"Okay enough about big dicks. I want to have a lunch today over here with you and mom."

"Why?"

"So that the two of you can clear the air and start to work on a future relationship."

"Jackie I don't know about that, it's been too long and too much pain."

"Please try for me, your only sister. I am your only sister right." They both laughed.

"Okay, but I can't make any promises."

"Alright, I will get started on it now. Get up and get dress. I know you can't be tired after lil man."

"You got jokes."

"By the way, I bought you something from the mall yesterday, I hope you like it."

"Thank you."

"You're very welcome."

Pamela walks into the kitchen to see if there was anything that she could do to help. As usual Jackie had everything under control. There was a beautiful salad on the table, several different dressings, garlic bread,

Lasagna and fresh lemonade. Who does that? Make
Lasagna for lunch. Jackie does.

"Who just has a pan of Lasagna hanging around?"
Pamela asks.

"Look at you. I knew you would look good in that
Wonder Woman halter and black shorts."

"I do look cute don't I?"

"Ya do! Remember you wanted to be and you would
wrap the towel around me to make me tell the truth."

"Yes and your dumb butt thought it was true. Where is
your Mandingo of a husband?"

"He just left to go play golf; he will be back in a couple
of hours."

Just then the doorbell rang. Pamela looked at Jackie
and took a hard swallow. Jackie took her hand and
kissed it and went to answer the door. Jackie opened
the door and she could see that her mother was nervous
too.

"Good morning mommy."

"Hey baby, how are you but its afternoon?" She smiled.

"I guess I'm a little nervous. I want the day to go well."

"Let's hope it does." She squeezed Jackie's arm.

They walk back to go join Pamela at the table. Pamela was already sitting at the table. When she saw her mother walking towards her, Pamela's skin began to each and she was rubbing her arms."

"Hello Pam."

"Hello, how are you?"

"I'm great. Excited to each lunch with my girls." She smiled at Pamela.

With everyone sitting at the table, they began to dig in and put the delicious food on their plates. It was still very awkward because no one was speaking just a lot of silver ware clinking. Pamela was feeling anxious because she really didn't want to have anything to do with her mother. She was only trying because of her sister.

"So Pamela, tell us what have you been doing with yourself." Mary asked.

"As far as what?"

"Like what you like and don't. Do you have a boyfriend? You know stuff like that."

Pamela was feeling so heated she wanted to explode. What have I been doing? Should I really say.

"I don't think you would really be interested in knowing."

"No baby I really would."

"Okay, since you sent me to live with my father. First thing was he trained me, by beating the hell out of me on a daily basis. Let me see he shot me up with heroin, oh yeah because he was my pimp. Oh but the kicker was, that he informed me that he wasn't even my father, that you were pregnant when you met. So you sent me to a man who wasn't even my dad, who became my pimp. Is there anything else you want to know?"

Jackie set there with her mouth open. She could not believe the horrible things her sister went through. She ran to hug her sister, but Pamela pushed her away.

"Pamela I am so sorry this happened to you." Jackie cried. "I'm sure mommy would not send you to a man like that willingly. Why would he lie about not being your dad?"

"Ask your mother?"

Mary was just sitting there shaking like a crazy. She never thought it would come out that he was not Pamela's father. Mary was afraid to open her mouth to speak.

"Mom you didn't send her there knowing that did you?" Jackie asked.

"I don't know why he did those things to you." Mary spoke.

"You are pathetic, who chooses a man over their child. Never check on them until the man that you chose died and now you want to be the best of friends. I can't stand you."

Mary slammed her hands on the table.

"I'm sorry. How many times do I have to say it Pamela!" She yelled.

Pamela stood up and slammed the table back.

"When in the hell did you ever say you're sorry? Never, I never heard from you when this man beat me, sold me and kept me doped up. Who is my father! Who is he! Do you even fucking know?" Pamela yelled back.

Mary was rocking back and forth holding her head. Jackie went over to hold her.

"It's ok mom, just tell her. So she can begin to heal as well as you."

"Yeah mom, tell me who my father is."

"I was raped. I don't know who your father is." Mary said.

"Wow can this day get any better. I'm done with you. So instead of telling me that, you send me to a rapist. You knew how he was. I saw this man beat you and make you have sex in front of me and you send me to him." Pamela sobbed.

"I'm sorry Pamela."

"Keep your pathetic sorry, forreal go kill ya self."

"Pam you don't mean that." Jackie pleaded.

"Yes, Yes I do." Pamela walked away.

"Please please Jackie take me home." Mary begged

"Mom I don't think you should be alone."

"I just want to go lay down."

"Mom you can go lay down in my bed."

"No I really want to go home."

"Okay."

7 THE DEATH OF A RELATIONSHIP

Pamela's head was killing her when she heard a knock at the door. Some guy was yelling Jackie's name. So Pamela went to the door and opened it. It was Gerald drunk as hell. He was being held up by one of his military boys.

"Hi I'm Xavier, is Jackie in."

"No I'm her sister, what is wrong with Gerald."

"He had a little too much to drink." He laughed.

"A little, can you put him in the bedroom down the hall and to the right?"

"Not a problem ma'am."

"It's just Pamela."

"Sorry it's the military in me."

Gerald began singing and grabbing Pamela's arm.

"Hey babe, I love you in that Wonder Woman shirt, it's hot."

"It's me Pam and your breath is dead boy." She laughed.

Xavier threw Gerald on the bed and Pamela walked him back to the door.

"Don't tell Jackie I brought him home like this because she will be so pissed at me."

"Your secret is safe with me."

Pamela walked back to the room to take Gerald's shoes off and cover him up before Jackie got home. One argument was enough for today. His feet were huge and he was heavy. Pamela was trying to cover him up when he started to caress her. He was rubbing her face and tried to kiss her. She pulled away.

"Gerald it's me Pamela, not Jackie."

"Baby your skin is so fucking soft, bring those breasts to me."

"Gerald stop." Pamela pushed him back.

He grabbed her by the arms as she tried to get up and pulled her onto the bed. Gerald pulled off her shirt and began sucking her breast, kissing her neck. Pamela began to moan and she knew it was wrong to allow this, she loved it. He instructed her to pull off her shorts and she did. Pamela got on top of Gerald and started to ride him. It felt so good and he did have a huge dick. Gerald was loving it and flipped Pamela over and started fucking her from behind. All Pamela could do was cum. Gerald couldn't understand why Jackie was not screaming, but didn't ask because she was throwing her hips which was new for her. He loved it. Gerald had finally exploded and Pamela quickly got up and put her things on in fear her sister would catch her.

"Hey babe, can you get me something to drink? You killing me." He laughed.

Pamela ran out of the room and straight to hers. Just in time she heard the key being turned and she jumped in her bed pretending to be sleep. Next thing there was a knock at the door.

"Hey are you okay?" Jackie asked.

"Yeah I'm good. What took you so long?" she asked.

"I had to go clear my mind. I went to walk at the River Front after I dropped mom off."

"I'm sorry about that."

"No apologies necessary, I understand why. I'm going to lay down for a couple of hours and then we are going out for a drink."

"Speaking about drinking, your husband is in the room passed out drunk."

"Really, who brought him home? Xavier?"

"I don't know who it was." She lied.

Jackie got up and headed towards her room. Pamela was so scared that Jackie would notice Gerald in the bed half naked and figure out she had sex with him. She waited and Jackie never came back so she went to sleep. Two hours later there was another heavy knock at the door, like the police. Pamela jumped out the bed and ran to the door. She opened it and it was William in his uniform. Jackie was hitting Gerald in his side.

"Someone is banging on the door like the damn police. Get your drunk ass up."

"Okay babe, damn you changed out of that Wonder Woman shirt quick." Gerald laughed.

"I don't have a shirt like that, I gave that to Pamela she is wearing that. Never mind that let's go see if someone is breaking in our house fool."

They get up and go into the living room where the police officer from the airport was standing hugging Pamela.

"Hey man you couldn't wait to see Pam huh?"

"How are you doing today Sir?"

"Sir? Aren't we a little formal?"

Jackie sees that Pamela is crying and he was actually holding her.

"What's wrong Pamela?" Jackie asks.

"Ma'am can you please have a seat?" William instructs her.

"What the hell is going on?" Gerald asks.

"It's your mother Mary, we got a call from a neighbor about a disturbance in her building and she shot herself."

"What! No this can't be true." Jackie screamed.

Jackie fell to her knees screaming. Gerald was trying to pick her up. Then Jackie turned to Pamela.

"Are you happy now? You told her to kill herself."

"I didn't mean it."

"Get out, Get the fuck out. I don't ever want to see you again."

"Pam its best you leave." Gerald told her.

Pamela went to gather her things. William told her she could come with him. She was leaving and wanted to give Jackie a hug but Gerald stopped her.

"I don't think this is the time right now."

Pamela turned around to leave, she hugged Gerald. William picked up her bags and she left. That's when Gerald recognized that smell and when she stepped back he seen the Wonder Woman halter.

****

"Mom, I can't listen to anymore." Monique stared at her.

"I just wanted you to know what her life was truly like."

"Wait, so….. Keysha and I are." She paused

"Yes, your sisters." Jackie told her.

"Ain't this about some shit, history constantly repeating itself." She got up and walked away.

8 COVERING UP LIES

Harmony has been texting Treasure all night, with no answer. She knew that she probably left with the doctor last night as she often did. Harmony knew that Treasure was fucking that good old doctor. She loved to hear about how they would have crazy sex all around the hospital without ever getting caught. Harmony figured she was at his cabin in the mountains that no one knew of. Her phone was vibrating. It was a text, hopefully from Treasure.

"Hey babe, WYD?" it said.

It was just her boyfriend Tristan. He was a 6'2" with pearly whites and that gorgeous football body. She met him her freshman year at school and she loved him. He was so attentive and loving. He was always so manicured, even more put together that her at times, she texts him back.

"Nothing, stressed. Looking for Treasure."

"Don't worry boo; I got you if you need me."

"I definitely need you." She smiled.

"Can we meet up tonight?"

"Yes, when and where."

"My place around 6."

"Be there."

"Love you."

"Love you more."

Then another text came through and it was Treasure.

Harmony was so happy she could barely open the text.

"Hey sis, I am at the gym getting ready to box, do you want to meet for lunch at 1."

"Yes, I do. Where?"

"Justins"

"KK"

Treasure sits in the women's locker room with her face in her hands. She knew she had to get rid of some of this stress today. Treasure also understands she has to convince Harmony that she is still upset about her mom. Not to draw any attention to the way she is reacting. No one could find out that Keysha is still alive. She got up and walked out into the gym.

"Hey beautiful, you ready to box today." Jeff said

Jeff was her boxing trainer. He was a champion fighter and had been working with Treasure for about three years. He has been trying to convince her to go pro. Her technique was flawless and she was extremely quick. "You know it coach, lets kick some ass."

Treasure got in the ring with her sparring partner. Her mind was not on the workout. She was thinking about how her mother was killed, why her dad would treat her like that and never apologize for it? She began to strike her opponent. Power punch after power punch. Jeff is looking at her from the side of the ring. He knew something wasn't right and Alicia the sparring partner was in trouble. Treasure was giving Alicia severe body shots. Alicia was waving to end it, but Treasure kept going. Her mind was on last night. What if she wasn't working at the hospital on this particular night? What if her mother didn't continually sacrifice herself for everyone? Where would they be?

"Treasure okay that's enough?" Jeff yelled.

She continued to beat Alicia. Alicia had blood coming from her face and bent over screaming in pain. Jeff had to grab her and physically pin her to the ground.

"Jeff what the fuck are you doing!" She screamed.

"No what the fuck is you doing!"

"What, trying to box?"

"No the fuck you not, look at Alicia."

She looked up and it was the gym medics in the corner looking at her injuries. Alicia wasn't fully conscious. Blood was coming from her mouth and nose. She was moaning holding her stomach.

"What happened?" She asked.

"You don't remember??" He looked at her.

"I did that." She began to cry.

"Treasure what is going on?" He asked her

"A lot, I can't get into it right now."

"Well you need to take care of it, because you may have just killed Alicia."

They both got up and walked over towards Alicia. Everyone in the gym was looking at Treasure with fear in their eyes. She felt so uncomfortable. She swallowed hard and stood by Jeff as he spoke to the medics.

"Todd, is she okay." He asked

"Man barely, she has broken ribs, broken nose and a cut across her eyes. This is on the outside." Todd looked at Treasure.

"I'm sorry Alicia, I don't know what came over me. I'm sorry."

"She can't hear you because she is in so much pain." He said sarcastically.

"Ok Todd." Jeff spoke

"Ok, Todd my ass. This nut almost killed this girl." He walked away.

"I think you should leave Treasure and I will contact you when you can come back." Jeff said to her.

"What, I didn't mean to hurt her." She said

"But you did." He said.

She walked away feeling horrible. She made her way towards the locker room and looked back. They had the stretcher for Alicia and all eyes were on her. She wanted to just punch the wall for being so dumb.

"Breathe." She told herself

Now to get her story straight before she goes to see Harmony and hopefully no charges will be pressed

9 JAIL VISITATIONS

Davon sat in his cell smiling. He knew today was the day that Asia would come to see him. He was sleeping with Asia before he got locked up for Keysha. She was so loyal to him and she proved it time and time again. Asia would put money on his books, send him anything he needed and take care of any people he felt hurt him. He looked over to his wall with pictures of Monique, Harmony and Treasure. He loved them so, but he still hated Keysha. He was thinking to himself the one bitch he couldn't tame.

"Hey Day, it's almost that time." Jug said.

"Ok, yes. Lemme see what I can get us today." Davon laughed.

Jug was his cellmate and part time lover. Davon believed if a man sucked your dick but don't penetrate you and it was also his cousin, then you're not gay. Jug was a big dark brown, over muscular man who was in jail for murdering his best friend for stealing his money during his drug dealer days. He had long braids that he had done by what they call the cell block house bitch. The first year Davon was in jail he never thought about touching another man. His cousin protected him and showed him how to defend his self and inject fear into the inmates. So around year three and realizing he wasn't going to ever leave this place, he gave in to temptation.

"Hey Jug, how do you let another nigga suck you dick? So does that mean you gay?" He asked.

"No mutherfucker. Not if you don't let them fuck you in the ass." He said.

"Man I'm horny as shit but I ain't gonna let nobody suck my dick in here." He laughed.

"Oh you laugh, huh? Oh you not? How many years you got? That's right life bitch." Jug laughed.

"Man that shit is gay yo." He yelled

Jug punched him in the face and he fell on the floor. Davon jumped up and squared up. He knew he couldn't beat his cousin, but he was going to try it.

"Yo you want these hands for real." Jug put his fists up.

Davon thought about the guy his cousin almost killed and that was with no effort really. He thought if he became on bad terms with his cousin, that it will be hell for him on this block because his cousin ran the block. "Nah man. We family, I don't know what I was thinking." He put his hands down.

Jug still had his hands in the air. He wasn't sure he should let this one slide. It was still his first cousin and they had the same grandma. So he put his hands down. Davon put his hands out to dap him up. Jug dapped him and brought him in for a chest bump.

"Nigga don't try that shit again. I have to remain the top dog here. Killing you will keep me there. Who kills their own cousin?" He pushed him.

Davon knew he wasn't playing and felt that he was on his cousin shit list. Somewhere that was damn near impossible to get off of.

"Don't be like that cuz; this place will make you lose your mind." He tried to smile.

"Ok, don't let this place catch you a body bag." He told him.

"I gotcha." He felt relieved.

"Now we got that out of the way. Take your pants off." He told Davon

"For what?" Davon was nervous.

"Really, take your shit off and don't let me tell you again." He got close to his face.

Davon was real hesitant. What was Jug going to do to him? He figures he was going to beat him for disrespecting him. Well at least it's dark in here and no one can see him get his ass whipped and he wouldn't make a noise just take it like a man. He took off his pants.

"Them draws to nigga." He pointed

Davon was terrified, but he didn't show any fear. He was just hoping that he didn't break anything. Jug walked towards him. Davon closed his eyes and took a deep breath. He started to feel warm and began to moan. He looked down and Jug was sucking his dick.

"Jug what are you doing?" He asked

Jug kept going, sucking Davon's dick. Davon wanted to push him away but it felt so good. He was feeling conflicted this is his cousin, a man and does this make him gay. Jug was going in and Davon finally nutted.

"You feel better?" he asked.

"I don't know how I feel." Davon quickly grabbed his clothes.

"I told you it don't make you gay, nigga." Jug told him

"I guess."

"Now get on your knees and repay the favor. All throat no teeth nigga." Jug said.

****

Davon heard Jug calling him. He was just staring off in space.

"Davon its visiting hours come on." Jug said

"Oh shit here I come." Davon said

"What the hell was you thinking about?" He asked

"Just something I wish I could forget, it's not important." He said.

Davon walks down the dark and damp hallway to the visiting area. He hated the way he was treated, shackled, searched. He truly felt he did nothing wrong and Keysha got what she deserved and he should be free. He walked in the room and he saw Asia sitting at the table waiting for him. She was so beautiful, but he could really care less about her. She had beautiful braids in her hair, cute little jeans that showed her perfect shape and a gorgeous smile. His heart belonged to Monique, so it was non-effective.

"Hey shorty!" He said.

"Oh my gosh Davon." She went to hug him.

The guard started to walk towards him. Davon pushed her back and motioned her to sit down. The guard stepped back.

"You know you can't be doing that shit, you trying to get me sent back before the visit is over." He told her

"I'm sorry but I just wanted to touch you." She said

"I know but we can't do that, plus I will try to slide my fingers in when it gets a little bit more crowded, ok." He smiled at her.

"Umm that sounds so good right now; it's hard to be a good girl with you in here." She told him

"I told you go ahead get yours, I'm in here for life. I don't expect you to suffer. I do expect you to take care of me while I'm in here thou."

"I got you daddy."

"So when did you get out." He asked her.

"I'm fresh out two weeks." She told him

"So did you handle that business for me?"

"Yes, I did."

"So what happened?" He asked her

"I did exactly what you said, I befriended her." She told him

"So." He became anxious.

"I set her up and the crew stabbed her." She told him

"Well, is she okay or is she?"

"She didn't make it." She looked sad.

"What the fuck is wrong with you?" He asked her

"I don't understand why you didn't like her. She was really cool and she was the mother of your daughter." She said.

"You don't need to understand! That bitch ruined my life and I only have on daughter, her name is "Harmony"." You hear me.

"Yeah, what the fuck is wrong you?" She was surprised by his tone.

"Nothing."

"So what about those fingers, it's crowded." She smiled

"Nah, I'm good." He got up and signaled the guard to leave.

Asia was shocked. She didn't understand why he was acting like that. She sat there for a few minutes as she got herself together. Her eyes were burning as she tried to not cry. She was wondering how a man that is locked up could affect her like this. She got herself locked up for him and gets Keysha killed for him and this is the thanks she gets. She was done with him and she was going to see the very daughter he hated and tell everything.

Davon walked up to the guard. He turns around so he can go the same degrading procedures to return back to his cell.

"Turn back around yo." The guard said

"What?" Davon asked him

"You have another visitor." He pointed

He didn't even want to turn around. He was hoping it wasn't Asia being difficult. He was done with her and he was going to let that ass have it. He turned around slowly and it was Mr. Walker, his attorney. What was he doing here? Can't be good news at all?

"Mr. Walker, what are you doing here?" Davon asked

"I have some news for you." He smiled.

10 XAVIER THE BUSINESS MAN

Xavier is sitting in his office feeling angry. Monique has never acted like that before. He didn't know how to approach her. He didn't have time to think about that right now, he had a meeting in ten minutes with the CEO of a huge job placement company.

"Mr. Baptiste your 10 O'clock is here." His secretary informed him.

"Thank you Rosa."

He took a deep breath and stood up and headed towards the door.

"Mr. Matthews." He said.

"None of that Mr. Matthews. Its Morris." He stretched out his hands.

"Ok, Morris." He shook his hand

Xavier motioned him over to the table with two plush leather seats. Morris thought this man is making money. The wall where the table sat was beautiful glass from head to toe. It was so luxurious.

"Please have a seat." Xavier said to him

"Thanks for meeting with me." Morris said.

"Ok let's get down to business." Xavier went straight in.

"Can you explain a little how this works and how I would get paid?"

Xavier grabbed him off his seat and pinned him up against the glass. He had a hand device and he pushed it. Suddenly two big buff, muscular guys ran in with guns drawn. Morris didn't know what was going on. He was scared and his heart was beating very fast. He was trying to speak and couldn't get anything out. He was stuttering.

"What, What in the hell is going on? Morris said.

"Nigga you the fucking feds." He put his elbow in his throat.

Before he could speak, the two guys had a gun to his head. He didn't know what was going on. Yet he knew to answer each question very carefully but quickly. He just wanted to make some extra money and nothing else.

"No I'm not." He spoke.

"Boss watch out let me search him real quick." He said.

"Yeah do that." Xavier said to him.

Xavier took his elbow off his neck. Morris bent down as to take in deep breathes. The guy snatched him up and made him stand up. Morris didn't put up a fight. This guy was 6'6 and an easy 350lbs and black as ever. He was so afraid, was he going to make it out of this meeting. Morris was made to strip all the way down to his draws and the guy search them too.

"He good boss." He said to him.

"I'm sorry I had to do that, but trust don't really exist anymore." He lit his cigar.

"What is really up?" Morris asked.

"Do you still want to make some money?"

"You damn right." Morris said.

"Ok, this is what I need from you." Xavier explained to him.

As they sat at the table, Morris started to have second thoughts. He was all in now and he couldn't pass up $25,000 a month. Morris started thinking of all the shit he could do with this fast money and all he had to do was supply a hotel floor and that was it. As Xavier gave him very detailed instructions on what to do. He made it very clear to follow these instructions exactly as he says or there would be consequences for his insubordinate behavior. Xavier assured him that he would be in contact with him and then the guys walked him to the elevator. As the doors opened it was Monique.

"Good afternoon Mrs. Baptiste." They both said.

"Hi Marco and Blaze. The name is Monique." She smiled.

They both laughed and moved to the side so she could exit the elevator. As she walked by, Morris was staring at her. Monique was so sexy, she had on a white dress on with royal blue high heels with the fringe on them swaying back and forth as she walked.

"I don't believe I have met you before." She smiled.

"Hi Monique, I am Morris, a business associate of Xavier's." He smiled

"Oh so you are in business with my husband, he is doing such a great job placing individuals with employment." She smiled

"Yes he is."

She walked away and they were all staring at her thick ass. Blaze and Marco pushed Morris on the elevator. Before the elevators closed, Blaze slapped Morris on the back of the head for looking at Monique.

Monique walked up to Rosa. Rosa was on the phone and put one finger up to signal she was going to be right with her.

"Monique, hi." She jumps up.

"Rosa baby," she hugged her.

"I haven't seen you in forever."

"You know Xavier hates when I come to his job. He says I'm a distraction."

"Well he's in. He just finished with his meeting." She said.

"Good, I caught him and he's not busy."

"I didn't say all that, I can let him know you're out here." She laughed

"No that's ok. I want to surprise him."

She cracked the door slowly and she sees Xavier gazing out of the window. Monique wondered what he was thinking about, where was his mind at. She walked up behind him and slid her arms around his waist. He turned around in a panic. She laughed....

"Oh, shit Monique you scared the shit out of me" He smiled at her.

"Yes, you were a million miles away." She caressed his face

"You know work and you." He kissed her on the forehead.

"I know, that's why I am here. To apologize to you."

"No apology necessary, I just want you to be ok." He said

"Oh I am baby." She slid her hands down his shoulders. Xavier looked at her and she had a different look in her eyes, He was confused, was she really okay.

"What?" she said.

"I don't know, are you sure you're okay?"

Just at that moment Monique slowly slid down to her knees and unbuckled his belt and slid his pants and boxers down. She grabbed his penis and began sucking it. He was shocked because Monique was a little reserved in the bedroom. He began to moan and through his head back. She knew she had to go the extra mile today to put plan in motion.

"Baby, I don't understand." He moaned out.

Monique continued to please him to the point he could no longer take it. He wanted to fuck her right there. She knew she had to control the situation.

"Step out of those pants and take off that shirt." She commanded

He was stunned at how direct she was with him. He didn't ask any questions and did what she said. His dick was hard as a rock and he just wanted to be in her. He walked to a fully clothed Monique.

"Stop right there." She put her hand up.

He didn't understand why she would stop him. She walked over to the door and locked it. She then picked up the phone and told Rosa to go to lunch and for no one to disturb Mr. Baptiste for about an hour. She turned around and Xavier was standing with a wonderful erect dick.

"Sit in that chair over there." She directed him.

He sat down in the cold leather chair with no arm rests. She walked up to him and stood just arm's length away from him. Monique slowly took off the form fitting dress. To reveal a well-toned body and black lace panty set. Xavier was about to bust, he started to move towards her. She motioned "no" by swaying her finger back and forth. She turned around and bent over swaying her ass back and forth as she began to take off her heels.

"No leave them on." He whispered.

She smiled and walked to him and slid her hand down his face. He began to suck her fingers. She took his hand and stuck his fingers inside her. Monique moaned and wet his fingers up. He couldn't take it anymore. Frankly neither could she. He went to get up, because he wanted to bend her over his desk like he had did many of his employees including Rosa. She pushed him back and he slid his pants off. Monique climbed on top of him in the chair. She began to bounce up and down nice and slow. He was just so happy to be inside of her. She then started a much faster paced rhythm and it felt just as good to her as him. Xavier was loving this new wife of his. He could no longer take it and exploded in Monique. He was breathing harder than usual.

"Are you ok?" She chuckled.

"Oh it's funny, that you almost killed me." He laughed

"You're ok. We needed this."

"Yeah I definitely did." He kissed her neck.

Xavier was so happy because his wife was present again. Xavier just held her close to him. Monique was kissing the top of his head. She got up and walked to the restroom located in his office. Xavier followed behind her. They were cleaning themselves up.

Monique started to look off into the distance.

"What's wrong?" He cupped her face.

"I'm worried about Treasure." She said.

"Yes, she's going through a rough time right now." He said

"Well, I called the hospital to check on her and they said she quit her job." She sighed.

"What? Have you spoken to her?"

"Harmony hasn't seen her, but they are meeting for lunch today."

"Babe if anyone can get through to her it's Harmony."

"I hope so."

"What else can we do?" He asked.

"You think you can give her a job here."

"Here!"

"Yes here. Is that a problem." She asked him.

"Um no baby, but I don't have any positions right now," he looked at her.

"You can't find her something." She rubbed his back. Xavier just thought about what just happened and how great the sex was. He definitely wanted it to continue. He wanted to make his wife happy, but she still didn't want her to know the nature of his business.

"I got you Hun," He hugged her.

She knew right then and there she had his ass.

11 MY COUSIN IS MY SISTER

The hostess seats Treasure at the outside patio of the Italian restaurant. It is a beautiful and warm day. A great day to be with her favorite cousin. She didn't know what she was going to say to her. Treasure had been dodging her and keeping this huge secret from her. They told each other everything. That's the only person that knew she was fucking the good ole doc.

"Ma'am would you like something to drink?" the waitress asked.

"Oh no thank you, I'm waiting for someone." Treasure smiled.

Harmony parked her jeep and was feeling so nervous, because she hasn't seen Treasure in a minute. She was contemplating telling her that her mom and aunt Keysha were sisters. They are sisters too and how messed up Treasures' grandmother, Pam, life was. She would just play it by ear. She walked up to the restaurant and saw Treasure sitting on the patio. She took a deep breath and started towards Treasure.

"Well hey stranger." Harmony smiled.

"Hey boo." Treasure smiled.

She stood up and gave her a long hug and had to hold back the tears she so desperately wanted to let flow. She was so much like Keysha. She didn't want to seem weak. Harmony pulled her close and they missed each other so much, that they both began to cry.

"Bitch we to cute to be crying out in public." Treasure laughed.

"Well we got the ugly cry thing going on right now." She snorted.

"True, Miss Piggy."

They began to laugh. Treasure and Harmony was so relieved there wasn't any awkwardness between the two. Yet, they both had secrets they need to tell. Harmony grabbed tissues and gave some to Treasure. She took her mirror out of her purse to fix her face.

"Vain hussy." Treasure said.

"You need to fix your tired ass face too," They laughed They were looking at the others face to make sure it looked good. Wiping the tears of the other.

"I'm sorry, would you like me to come back?" The waitress asked.

They looked up and began to laugh. The waitress didn't know what to think. She had a puzzling look on her face.

"Oh no were ready to order." Treasure said

"Yes, we just haven't seen each other in a while." Harmony said.

"That is usually how it is with sisters." The waitress said

"Yes, yes it is." Treasure smiled

"So what can I get you ladies?" She asked them

"I will start with a Pinktini and I will also have the seafood fettucine." Harmony said.

"Really?" Treasure looked up from the menu

"Yes I'm hungry, health buff." She laughed

"Ok but the Pinktini." She asked

"Yes, I'm a lady." She chuckled

"Well I will have your grilled salmon, asparagus and brown rice." She said.

"So boring." Harmony faked yawned

"Also I would like two shots of tequila, salted rim and two limes."

"Showing your ass are we??" Harmony giggled.

"Yes I am."

"Let the fun begin."

The waitress smiled and told them their food would be out shortly. She took the menus and walked away. Harmony touched Treasures hand.

"I really missed you." Harmony said.

"I missed you even more." Treasure squeezed her hand.

"So are you really ok?" Harmony asked.

"Absolutely! If shit wasn't on point you would be the first person that I would tell." Treasure looked away because she was lying and it was killing her. She knew she couldn't take a chance on anyone finding out about her mother.

"Ok, but I know your lying." Harmony raised her eyebrow.

"Stop with the eyebrow raise." Treasure puckered her lips.

"Ladies here are your drinks." The waitress set them down.

"Thank You." They both said.

"Well cuz, here's to us." Harmony picked up her drink.

"Nope wait, this drink is for you." Treasure hand her one of the tequila shots

"What?" Harmony laughed.

"Yes one for you and one for me, you know I'm not a drinker. Everyone thinks you're goodie. No one knows you're the drinker. Secret kept." Treasure gave her the thumbs up.

"Give it here trick, I love your simple ass."

"Back at you twin." She blows a kiss.

The clink glasses and down the shots. Treasure is feeling warm and comfortable. She really misses her cousin. Harmony is talking up a storm but she can't hear her because everything that is on her mind.

"So, what do you think about me doing that?" She asked

"Doing What?" Treasure asked her.

"Are you listening? You only had one shot." She laughed

"That's all it takes for me."

"I said my man wants to get married. What do you think?" She asked.

Treasure was shocked. She didn't dislike him, but a really good friend told her he was gay last week and she hasn't told Harmony yet. Now that she wants to marry him, she had to tell her.

"I'm shocked."

"Why, I know we haven't been together for long but I love him." Harmony smiled.

"That's the only dick you've been with, don't you want to make sure he's the only one you will be fucking the rest of your life." She asked.

"Well damn. I didn't say yes." Harmony was disappointed.

"I'm sorry; I just want you to be sure and take your time." She smiles.

"You're right, it just feels good to be loved and wanted."

"You're gorgeous and will always be wanted." She smiled.

"Ok, remember that I am older." Harmony said.

"I know you never let me forget."

The waitress sat their food down and as usual Harmony was taking food off Treasures plate, they laughed and reminisced. Harmony ordered four more Tequila shots. Treasure and Harmony were stinking drunk and the emotions began to pour out.

12 FREEDOM IS PRICELESS

Asia couldn't believe the call she just received from Davon. Could it be true? Was the wait finally over. All she could think about was being a family with the man she loved and even killed for, was coming home. When she got the call last night she was in shock.

"You have a collect call, from the Georgia Department of Corrections? The operator said.

Asia was so excited, because the last encounter with Davon did not go over very well. So she was hoping that he was not still mad at her. So, she quickly accepted the charges.

"Hello babe?" She said.

"Hey, what's up?" Davon said with excitement in his voice.

"I'm so glad you called, because you seemed so upset with me the last time I came to visit you."

"Yeah about that, I had a lot of shit on my mind." Davon told her.

"Ok well you should not treat your woman like that." She started to say but was interrupted.

"Look you want to argue about the that shit or do you want to come pick me up tomorrow?" He laughed.

"Davon what are you talking about?" She said.

"Well to make a long story, real short. My sentence has been overturned and I am free."

"How did this happen? Are you playing with me?" Asia asked.

"Look why the fuck would I play about some shit like that. Are you coming to get me tomorrow? So we can start our lives together?" He said to her.

"Oh my goodness, yes babe!" She became so excited.

"Ok, calm down. Listen this is what I need you to do." Davon said in a stern voice.

"Ok daddy, What?"

"I need you to be here around 9, I probably won't be done until around 12, but I want you here. Make sure you bring some money so I can get my hair cut and get some new clothes and a new cell phone. You hear me." He said.

"Of course baby, you know I gotcha." She said.

"Well I have to go; I have some loose ends to take care of. See you tomorrow." He hangs up.

"I love you baby." She said but Davon had already hung up the phone. She felt hurt, but told herself that he was so excite to see her that's why he hung up so quickly.

Just in that moment, Tristan walked in the door. He saw Asia sitting on the sofa crying. He walked over to her and put his hand on her shoulder.

"Hey sis, why are you crying? What's wrong? He said.

"Nothing these are happy tears." She said.

"Ok." He looked confused.

"My boyfriend is coming home and we are going to be a family now." She told him.

"The boyfriend that has been in jail for the last, I don't know, how many years." He rolled his eyes.

"Look, I love him and I want you to except him, when he gets home." Asia told him.

"What home? I know good and well damn hell, that jailbird is not coming here to live. Oh hell no!" He was pissed.

"Now wait one damn minute Tristan, this is my house and I..." She started to say, but was interrupted.

"Umm, get it straight this is our home. Our parents left it to us, remember that." He told her.

"Ok, our home. I want him here with me Tristan." She touched his hands.

"Why do you want someone that has been in jail for who knows what, because you still haven't told me why he was in jail." He looked at her.

"I told you he was falsely accused of a crime and it has been proven because he is getting out of jail tomorrow." She smiled.

"You are so dumb, you believe anything. He can come up in here and kill us." He glared at her.

"You are so over dramatic." She laughed.

"Was mommy and daddy over dramatic when they took in that foster kid and he repaid them by killing them in their sleep." He told her.

"They were sick, everyone is not a killer." She told him.

"Yeah ok, just keep him away from me. I'm sure he has a lot of secrets, he has yet to tell you." Tristan said.
"Well he is not the only one with secrets, is he?" She walked away.
"Harmony can change me!" He yelled at her.

****

Davon went back to his cell and was so happy in less than twenty-four hours he would be a free man. He was dreaming about having his family back with Monique and Harmony. He didn't care that she was married now. With Keysha being out of the picture, he could win her back. He never stopped loving her and he knew she had to feel the same way.
"What up cuz?" Jug said.
"Nothing, what up with you?" He said
Davon tries not to make eye contact with his cousin, because he is so disgusted by what he made him do. He hasn't told Jug he was getting transported off this block and placed in waiting because he was being released tomorrow. Jug knew something was up, because all of Davon's stuff was packed and laying on his bunk.
"You going somewhere?" Jug asked.
"Yeah yo, I'm being released." He said
"What you mean being released? Like yo ass is free." He asked him.
"Yeah." Davon started getting his stuff together.

"You could have told a nigga." He walked towards him.

"You never know if shit is true, so I said nothing." He laughed.

He walked up to Davon and gave him dap and a hug. Jug was pissed a little, he was going to be in prison until he died. He was wondering how this nigga got out. What was he doing? Davon didn't know how to take this.

"So you make sure to tell the family that I miss them and shit come see a nigga." He told Davon.

"I most definitely will." He breathed a sigh of relief. Just then jug grabbed him by the neck and began chocking him. Davon did not try to fight him, he wanted to make sure he was leaving and never coming back to this place again. Jug licked his face and started rubbing his dick.

"Shit one for the road cuz." He kissed him.

"Come on jug, I am not gay man." He told him

"If you leaving me man, I got to hit that just once for the road." Jug stuck his tongue in his ear.

"I'm not fucking gay!" He yelled hoping the guards would hear him.

"Ok, cuz you want to play. Either you suck my dick or I beat your ass and fuck the shit out of you. Either way, I'm coming today." He squeezed his neck even harder. Davon was so fucking pissed, but if he fought back. This could extend his stay he thought. Jug knew he had him and Davon was going to abide by what he said.

Davon dropped to his knees and took a hard swallow. He had to get his mind right. Jug pulled out his huge, black dick. Davon looked at the ground and felt like he was going to be sick. Why would his cousin do this to him?

"Davon, you don't have all day. Give some attention to my dick sir." He laughed.

Davon opened his mouth and Jug shoved his dick in his mouth. He began to gag and felt like he was going to throw up. He kept with the back and forth motion. Jug was moaning and rubbing his head.

"Yes, suck this dick boy. I think I want to fuck you in your ass." He said.

Davon became terrified and began sucking his dick even harder and faster, he wanted him to cum. He did not want to be raped in here, nor did he want stiches. Davon began rubbing his balls and Jug finally came. All on Davon's face and he rubbed his dick all over his face. Davon jumped up and threw up in the toilet. He was so mad, but couldn't do anything about it.

"Thanks, cuz I needed that." He wiped his hands so Davon's back.

Davon couldn't wait to get out of here and to never think about this day again. Freedom was hours away and he was not going to fuck it up for anyone. Just as he was finishing cleaning himself up, the guard came to the cell.

"Hey lets go." The guard said.

"Who me?" Jug said.

"No, him." Pointing to Davon

"You get up against the wall." The other guard said.
Jug got off the bunk and put his hands up against the wall. Davon grabbed his belongings, the cell doors opened and he walked through them and sighed. He never looked back at his cousin who just emasculated him. He was free, no more sucking any man's dick. Jug turned around once the cell doors closed. He was jealous, and hated Davon for getting his freedom.

"Ok, cuz make sure you write me and come see me." Jug said.

Davon kept walking and never looked back. He wanted Jug to feel the hate he had for him. He knew it would hurt Jug to not be acknowledged.

"Ok, bitch, fuck you! I want to thank you for that great blow job. I should have fucked your ass til it was bloody!" He yelled. "You fucking faggot!"

Davon was tempted to yell something back. He realized his freedom was the best revenge.

13 THE RISE OF A PHOENIX

Treasure was speeding to the cabin to see her mother. She is so happy that she is making a somewhat speedy recovery. Keysha is walking very well despite the stab wounds and the HIV meds have been doing a wonderful job. Treasure and Keysha hated lying, but had to for right now. Treasure's cell phone starts to ring and she hits talk on her car steering wheel.

"Hello Jeff, how are you?" Treasure said.

"I'm great, how are you?" He asked.

"I will be doing better if you tell me that I'm not going to jail." She laughed.

"Well I convinced Alicia not to press charges on you."

"Yes, thank you so much Jeff!" She said.

"Don't thank me yet, you are barred from the property." He told her

"Are you serious, where am I supposed to work out at?" Treasure asked him.

"Did you see Alicia's face? Did you really think I would let you come back? I like you and all but come on Treasure."

"Yeah, I guess you are right." She said.

"You can still come to the house and hit the bag, as long as you don't go off on me. You nut case you." He laughed.

"I promise." She laughed

"Ok talk to you later." He said

"Bye."

Treasure finally pulls up to the cabin and it is so breathe taking. She parks in the u-shaped drive way and turns of the car. This home has beautiful logs, a huge porch with four rocking chairs and huge clear glass door. The home is engulfed in huge trees, with moss hanging on each tree like Christmas tinsel. Keysha was sitting in the rocking chair wrapped up in a mink comforter, sipping tea. She was so happy to see her mom outside, even though Keysha had been recovering for several hours she had refuse to come out of the home. Keysha waves at Treasure. Treasure gets out of the car and walks on the cobble stone that leads to the steps.

"Hi Mom." Treasure kisses her on the fore head.

"Hi baby."

"How are you feeling today?" She asked her mom.

"I actually feel great." Keysha said

"I can tell cuz you're outside. And you're smiling." She grabbed her hand.

"Your doctor friend is taking really good care of me." She smiled.

"He damn well better be." Treasure looked serious.

"Stop it, he is really nice and we need him for now." She kissed her hand.

Neither knew that the doctor was standing in the door way. He looked at them, he couldn't stand either one of them. What could he do to get out of this situation? Treasure had him pinned in a corner. She knew every deep dark secret about him, that would cause him to lose his medical license. He could just kill both and bury them on his property no one would ever know about it. He chuckled to himself. Just at that moment, Keysha looked around Treasures waist and noticed his evil smile and he was lost in thought. She knew it would only be a matter of time before they would have to get rid of him. He stepped out onto the porch and walked towards both ladies.

"Good morning ladies." He said

"Good Morning Kai, how are you?" Treasure spoke to him.

"Kai, that's your first name?" Keysha asked.

"Yes, it is." He said.

"It's a nice name." Keysha said.

"Treasure, could I speak to you in private please?" Kai asked.

"That would be a no, anything you need to say, you can say in front of my mom." She told him.

Kai looked at Treasure he was pissed. He grabbed her hand and begun to squeeze it. I don't think Kai realize who he was fucking with, Keysha was thinking. It was nothing to her to shoot first and never ask questions. Treasure was her life and she would never lose her again. Keysha stood up.

"I will go in the house, so you can have a minute." She said.

"Mom, no. You don't have to go. It's no secrets between us." Treasure reassured her.

"Thanks, Keysha, I appreciate it." Kai said.

Keysha walks in the house slowly and gives Treasure a look. Treasure wasn't sure what that was about. Treasure walked over to the opposite side of the porch and sat in the chair and began to rock back and forth. Kai rubbed his head and began to speak.

"Treasure I'm just going to be straight with you." He said

"Straight with me about what?" Treasure asked him.

"I'm getting tired of you and your mom. I don't want to have nothing to do with this bull shit anymore." He said.

"Oh really?" She asked him.

"Yes, Oh really." He told her.

He noticed Treasure was looking as if what he was saying did not matter. She continued to rock in that chair. Kai was beginning to get angry. He was helping this bitch and she could careless and he was putting everything he had work for into jeopardy.

"Treasure I am not about to lose everything I work for, for you and your HIV infected mother." He said.

"Don't ever speak about my mother like that ever again because I will ruin everything you have or will ever try to acquire. Fuck with me and see!" She yelled.

Something went through Kai and he walked up to Treasure with a crazed look in his eyes. Treasure seen the look in his eyes and stood up. Kai had hauled of and slapped Treasure and she fell to the ground. Treasure was stunned and touched her face and her nose was bleeding. She jumped up and they began to fight and he was too strong to fight him off.

"Get off me, you punk bitch." Treasure tried to say but couldn't, Kai was choking her.

"Who's the bitch now? I'm going to kill you and then kill your mom. Then I can have my life back." He whispered in her ear.

Treasure was beginning to feel light headed and was afraid she would pass out. If he killed her all this would be in vain to save her mother. Just at the moment when she thought she would die. A shot rang out in the air. Treasure dropped to the ground, gasping for air.

"No Nigga, the only one dying today is you." Keysha said.

"Mrs. Keysha." Kai said.

"Mrs. Keysha my ass bitch! You hit my baby!" She yelled. Keysha pointed and pulled the trigger, hitting him in the left knee cap. He screamed and fell down to the ground.

Treasure, scared, jumped up and stood behind her mother. Kai was rolling on the ground screaming.

"Get your ass up." Keysha told him.

"I can't, you shot me." He whimpered.

"Really, I shot you. Yeah you not so bad now. Choking my fucking child." She told him.

"Mom." Treasure said.

"You better get up or I am pulling the trigger again." Keysha told him

"I'm getting up." Kai put his hands up

"Mom what are you doing?"

"We are going to take care of this nigga, its okay." Keysha said

Keysha and Treasure walked Kai into the woods behind his cabin. Kai was in so much pain and he was so terrified. Was he going to die. Where was she taking him? The path was familiar? Kai started thinking how would Keysha know this path. She couldn't be taking him there. Keysha marched his ass right through the woods. She knew the woods very well. Kai would leave every day at the same time and would be gone for hours. So, one day when he thought Keysha was sleep she followed him and what she saw was shocking. They had reached the area where he would escape to everyday for the last several weeks. Kai was shocked.

"Does this look familiar to you Kai?" Keysha asked him

"What is this place, mom?" Treasure asked

"Do you want to answer that question Kai?" Keysha asked

Treasure was confused and Kai was scared. The place where Keysha had taken him was to two grave sites he had dug for Keysha and Treasure. He had plans on killing both and burying them in this remote area. His planned has backfired. He attempted to run and Keysha shot him in the other leg.

"Oh baby, he was going to kill us, but I followed you every day." Keysha said

"You were going to kill me bitch? And my mother?!" She kicked him in the face.

"Yes, the graves you dug for me and my child. Will be filled with your body." Keysha told him.

Kai began to beg and plead for them to let him go. He was bleeding from the mouth where Treasure had kicked him. Kai was bleeding from both legs and couldn't move. He realized that he was going to die. There was no way out of it. Maybe if he told Treasure he loved her. Keysha walked over to the far tree to reveal the shovel he had been using to dig the graves.

"Treasure please, I love you. Don't do this." He pleaded.

"You love me? Didn't you just choke the shit out of me and was about to kill me and my mother???" She asked him

"We can leave and your mother can have the cabin and we will continue to get her medication." He begged.

"We both know she will get her meds. Thanks to you with the fake identity you purchased for her and I thank you." She smiled.

"I will make you happy." Kai attempted to win her over.

"I don't think so, too late. My mom is pissed now." She told him.

"Help! Help! somebody help me! "He screamed.

Keysha walks over to Kai and pulls the trigger twice to the head and just like that he was dead. Treasure jumped back, she had never seen a dead body. She had never killed anyone. The beating she gave Alicia, I guess she could be capable of that. Keysha threw the gun in one of the hole and motioned Treasure to help her with the body.

"Come on Treasure, let's put his ass in that hole and cover him up." Keysha said

"Mom you really killed him." Treasure stood there.

"Yes, I did. He was going to kill us Treasure." Keysha explained.

"You're right, him or us." Treasure said.

"And today it was him." She kissed Treasure.

14 HOME IS WHERE THE HEART IS

Davon was so excited to be leaving the prison behind him and Jug. As he walked out of the building he wanted to cry. Could it be true he was never going to have to take a shower with men again, he could eat what he wanted and he didn't have to look over his shoulder's anymore. The sun was beaming on his face and it felt good, the birds were chirping, he really didn't realize what he was missing being locked up for all these years. There was Asia leaning up against her black Range Rover, in a black maxi dress, with this beautiful blue jade necklace on. She ran up to him and hugged him. He hugged her back, but Monique was the only thing on his mind. She went to kiss him, but he pulled away.

"Babe, what's the matter with you?" She asked him

"Nothing I just want to get far away from this place." He told her

"Ok, I can understand that." She rubbed her hand up and down his arm.

"Can we get out of here, please?" Davon said

"Yeah baby, lets go." She smiled

While riding in the truck. It was a little awkward. Davon wasn't really talking to her. She began to wonder what he could have possibly be thinking of. She hopes it was about all the great times they were about to have. She loved him so much. Whatever it was, it had him captivated. She simply turned up the radio as Alicia Keyes "Like You'll Never See Me Again". As the song played, Davon thought about Monique was his everything and he wanted his family back. He wanted to hold her, tell her how sorry he was for hurting her and his daughter. He knew the first thing he would do would be to call her.

"Are you ok?" Asia asked him

"Yeah, I have a lot of shit on my mind." He told her

"You want to talk about it." She asked him

"No, Asia. Did you get me a phone?" He asked him

"Yes, I did Davon. I did damn." She felt hurt.

"What's your fucking problem?" He yelled at her.

"You." She said in a low tone

"Well we don't have to be together, drop me off at my mom's." He told her.

"It's nothing Davon." She said

"Good, because I don't need this shit right now." He told her

"Are you still coming with me to my house?" She asked him

"Yes Asia, Yes damn!" He yelled at her.

"Sorry Davon, I was just asking." Asia said

"Did you bring me those clothes?" He asked her

"There in the back." She said

"Yes, now drop me off at my mom's." He said

Asia was so hurt, she was fighting back tears. She pulled up to the brick rancher and Davon got out. He told her he would call her when he wanted her to pick him back up. Davon never even invited her to come in and meet his mother. She has never met her, she had been dealing with him for over fifteen years. When Davon got out of the truck, there were balloons everywhere, welcome home signs and his mom running towards him. He was so happy to see his mother, that he never seen cousins or him and Jug's grandmother. Asia sat for a couple of minutes then pulled off crying.

"My baby is home." His mother said

"That's right mom I'm home, for good." He kissed her on the forehead.

"Everyone is here, Mickey, Jo-Jo." She said

"What about Monique and Harmony?" He asked

"She wouldn't take my calls. You know she is married now." She told him.

"I don't care about that nigga mom, we will always be connected." Davon said.

She knew her son was still deeply in love with her. She didn't want him to get hurt. His mom motioned him up to the house to see the rest of the family. They were so happy to see him. His cousin's and his grandmother hugged him so tight, then she asked about how Jug was doing. He started to cringe. He told her he was doing fine and quickly changed the subject. It felt good to be home. He walked to the backyard and it was crowded with friends, family and old girlfriends but no Monique. Davon's mom had thrown him a bar b cue and it smelled great. Hamburgers, steak, hotdogs and soda. Davon was in heaven, but someone was still missing. He was determined to see her and get his family back.

Asia was so upset, she was crying so hard she began to gag. Her phone began to ring to the car and was her boss. She had to get it together, because the life-style she has been trying to live for her and Davon is costly. She was hoping he didn't want her to come in today, of all days not today. She got herself together and answered.

"Hello." She said

"Hi Asia, how are you?" He asked

"Hello, Mr. Baptiste." She said

"We so formal, Mr. Baptiste huh." He laughed

"Sorry about that, what's up?" She said

"Ok, Ghetto girl. I need you to come in today. I need to talk to you." He told her

"Right now." She asked

"Yes, you are my best girl. I need you to take care something for me." He demanded

"Ok, on my way." She ends the call.

Davon was nervous, he had gotten Monique's phone number from his mother. She had also given him the address so he could see Harmony. Would she allow him to see their daughter? He picked up the phone and took a deep breath and dialed the number.

"Hello." Monique said

"Hello." She said again

"Monique?" Davon said

"Yes, this is Monique." She said

"This is Davon." He cleared his throat

There was a paused, which seemed like forever. He was hoping this wasn't a mistake. Monique was in shock. She hasn't thought about Davon in years. Why would he be calling her? How is he calling her? She thought to herself that he wasn't calling from a prison. He couldn't be free she thought.

"Davon, why are you calling me?" She said

"I want to talk to my daughter." He told her

"Again, why are you calling me?" Monique said

"I just told you, I want to talk to Harmony." He told her

"Look, Harmony is grown and you can contact her directly." She said

"Does she still live with you? I want to stop by and see her." Davon told her.

"How would you be able to do that from behind bars?" She said to him

"I'm not behind bars. I'm home Monique." He told her

"Home. How?" She asked

"I want to see you and tell you what happened." He asked her.

"Meet, I. Davon I." She couldn't speak.

"Monique, I know it's a lot but I need to talk to you." He told her.

"I have to call you back, I can't talk right now." She told him.

"Ok. This is my cell number and I'm staying at my mom's house." He said

"I have to go." She hung up.

****
*

Monique sat on the edge of her beautiful king size bed in shock. Was this really happening. Why would anyone let him out of prison, after what he did? She just couldn't understand it. She had to talk to her husband, she needed his advice about this one. She grabbed her purse and keys of the nightstand and ran down the steps and out the door. She jumped in her truck and sped out of the driveway. She turned the music down and put her hand over her chest. She just could not believe that he was home. Davon was her first love and he also hurt the only person that truly loved her in a non-judgmental way her cousin Keysha. She wished Keysha was still alive so she could call her and tell her about this shit. She wanted to call her dad in Ohio, but he has been sick a lot lately and she didn't want him to worry. Off in the distance she heard someone beeping their horn. The light had turned green and she hadn't noticed it. The white man in his little red sports car, pulled up beside her and gave her the finger and passed her, Monique finally pulled off and was on her way to her husband's office.

Asia pulls up in front of the office building, she did not want to work today. She sighs and gets out of her jeep and heads in to the office building. Her heels are clicking against the marble floor as he walks towards the elevator. She gets in and pushes the seven and thinks herself to the top. She steps off the elevator and heads to the receptionist.

"Hi Rosa, I'm here to see Mr. Baptiste." She said

"Go ahead Asia, he is waiting for you." Rosa told her

Asia walked in the room and Xavier was standing by the floor length window on the phone handling business. She had to admit, he looked so handsome and powerful standing their commanding respect. His body was looking so good in the form fitting suit. She had to catch herself she started to warm all over. She checked herself out in the mirror to make sure she looked good, and she did. She clears her throat and Xavier turns around and waves her over with a big smile.

"How are you Miss?" He smiled at her.

"I'm great Xavier, how are you?" She looked at him.

There was a knock on the door and Rosa came in. She looked at them and they looked strange as if she had walked in on something.

"Boss I am going to lunch; did you need anything before I leave." She asked

"No, Rosa I'm fine. Look take the rest of the day off. With pay and start your Friday off now." He said

"Well thank you, I will." She smiled

 "Could you just lock the door on your way out?" He asked

Rosa was in such a hurry to get off work early, she had forgotten to lock the door. She pulled it tight and grabbed her purse and headed to the elevator.

"So back to why I brought you here." He said to Asia

 "I am just a little intrigued." She said.

 "I'm just going to be straight with you." He said

 "I wouldn't expect you to be any other way." She said

 "I need some more girls. I have a contract with hotel and we have some high-class gentlemen coming through. We can make some good money." He said

"How many girls? What race?" She asked him

"I need at least ten, all flavors and they must be fucking flawless." He said

"Don't I always deliver?" She said.

"Also, I need like two dudes. Can you make that happen?" He asked

"Damn Xavier, really. Yeah I think I can do that." She said

"What about your brother? They loved him." Xavier looked at her

"I will ask him, and see if he has any friends willing to get paid." She told him.

"My girl, as long as you keep recruiting. You don't have on lay on your back." He told her

"I will never lay on my back for money again. If I'm fucking it's because I want to." She told him

He walked past her and slapped her on her ass. Xavier has been fucking Asia for years and nobody knew it. Asia starting feeling wet between her legs. She told herself the last time she fucked him it was the last time. Eric grabbed her by the neck and put her hand on his dick and it was rock hard. He pushed her head back and started kissing her neck. Asia began to moan and she knew she was definitely getting fucked today. If Davon didn't want this pussy, she knew Xavier did. She began rubbing his back and slowly grabbing his dick and Xavier loved it.

"We fucking today?" She asked him

"Why you think I sent Rosa home early?" he asked

"Is it the usual?" She asked him

"What's the usual?" He looked at her

"You beating me today?" She looked at him

"Um, no and I'm sorry about that." He said

The last time they Xavier had sex with her, he took of his belt and beat her on ass with it. She was taken back at first, but it had turned him on so much. That she herself became turned on. Her ass was so sore from that and bruised she didn't know if she could do that again.

"No we just fucking today." He grabbed her.

Xavier pulled Asia closed to him and slid her dress to the floor. Asia started to take her necklace off, but he stopped her, he loved the way it looked on her neck. He looked at her body and young and beautiful it was. He loved his wife, but Asia exuded youth. Her breast just sat up on there on, her belly ring and the tattooed flowers running down her back. He grabbed her and began kissing her. Asia ripped off his shirt and began biting his nipples. Xavier quickly stepped out of his shoes and began pulling his pants off. He walked over to his desk to get a condom. On the way over to Asia he picked up the remote to play some music. He had it blasting, he knew that nobody else would be on the floor, his office was the only one. The door had been locked and he had no appointments today.

Asia had taken off the rest of her clothes and was bent over the sofa. She knew Xavier loved it from behind and so did she. He put his arms around her waist and licked her back, she started moaning. He blind folded her with his tie and put the condom on. He put his dick inside her and she was warm and wet. It took everything in him not to cum upon entering Asia. She loved the way he fucked her, He would go in deep and grab her by the throat at the same time. Xavier loved to blind fold her; he loved for Asia to be in suspense of when he would enter her. Xavier was stroking and stroking. Asia was sucking his fingers and Xavier wanted to cum so bad. He started slapping her ass and pulling her hair. She let Xavier treat her anyway he wanted to because she felt loyalty to him.

Monique rushed into the building and walked fast to the elevator. She knew Xavier would not believe this shit. Davon had the nerve to try and come back into her and Harmony's life. Hell, no she was not about to let that happen. She really needed her husband to lean on right now. She steps off the elevator and it is ghost and all she could hear is loud music playing. Rosa was nowhere in sight. She stood at the receptionist desk and everything was off, did Rosa leave for the day? She walked to the door and knocked. There was no answer. She knocked again. Monique knew Xavier had to be in there. Normally she would not bother him, but she was to upset. She reached for the door handle and twisted the knob. She opened the door and slowly peeped in. Monique could not believe her eyes. He husband was fucking another woman. Xavier never seen Monique standing there. His head was thrown back as he was moaning and the woman had a blind fold on. Monique closed the door and began to cry. She ran to the elevators and began to rapidly push the down button. She got on the elevator and slid to the floor with her hands over her mouth crying. The elevator reached the lobby and she stumbled out of the elevator and walked out of the building. She got in her truck and began to scream and beat on the truck steering wheel. Her phone began to vibrate, it was a text message. It was from Davon.

She started up her truck and started driving. Monique was in a daze, she couldn't believe what she had just seen. Her husband fucking another bitch. Why would he do that? She wanted Keysha back so badly. She continued to drive. Monique pulls up in the driveway and gets out. She walks up to the door and knocks. Davon opens the door. She looks terrible and he could tell she was crying. He grabbed her hand and pulled her in and began hugging her. They walked to the bedroom.

"What's the matter Mo?" He asked

She put her arms around his waist and began kissing him. Davon dick became so hard. He wanted this. Monique walked to the bed and took off her top and Davon closed the bedroom door.

15 REALITY SETS IN

Monique stands in her stoned shower. She is in disbelief of what just happened; did Xavier really just cheat on her? She just let the six-head shower of hot water hit her all over her body. She couldn't believe she let Davon fuck her like that. Monique had to admit she loved it, if Xavier didn't care why should she? She felt bad because she knew it was wrong and she still loved her husband. Monique just let her head hang down as the water ran down her back.

"Monique." Xavier called her but she did not answer him.

"Monique." He touched her back and she jumped.

"Shit Xavier! You scared me." She told him.

"Babe, I called you twice." He rubbed her back, she pulled away.

He looked confused. Why would she pull away from him? Then he noticed that she had been crying. He grabbed her hand and pulled Monique close to him. Xavier was still in his suit. He wrapped his arms around her and kissed her wet hair. Monique squeezed him tightly and little did he know; he was the reason for the tears.

"What's the matter Mo?" he asked her.

"It's been a long crazy day." Monique told him.

"Babe, I'm here for you, what happened?" Xavier lifted her head up by her chin.

"Davon is out of prison and he called me today." She told him

"What did that nigga want?" Xavier looked serious.

"He wanted to see Harmony." She told him.

"Forreal babe, let her make that decision to see him or not." He told her.

"He brings me so much pain, when I think about my cousin and the life she could've had if he didn't do that to her." She began to tear up

"How did that bum get out anyway?" He asked.

"I don't know, but he is out." She told him

"I tell you what if he comes around, that's his ass. I'm not playing with him. He will not mess up our home. It's just now getting back on track." He told her

"Get out of the shower, before you ruin your nice suit." She forced a smile.

"I'm already in here, so let's make the best of this alone time." He kissed her.

He took off his clothes and threw them on the floor and walked up to her. As they stood under the rain shower head, he began to kiss her. She didn't want to have sex with him knowing that he just had sex with some random girl. Xavier began to kiss Monique on her neck. She started to forget about today and just enjoying her husband. Xavier started to feel so guilty for cheating on his wife, especially because she is so faithful and loyal to him. He vowed to himself that everything from here was going to be business only.

"Baby, I'm sorry." He told her

"Sorry about what." She asked him

"I'm just not proud of about something I did today; I promise you I will never do it again. I don't want to go into details." He began to cry

She knew exactly what he was talking about. Monique couldn't believe it. Their entire marriage he never cried, except at his mother's funeral. She knew he was sorry and at that moment she forgave him. She wanted to come clean too, but couldn't. He never had to know, just as he never wanted her to find out about his side bitch.

"Babe, I forgive you." She kissed his hands

"You don't even know what I did." He looked at her.

"Whatever it is, I'm sure if I did the same, you would forgive me." She told him.

"I don't know if I could." He looked at her strangely. Monique cut the conversation short. She grabbed the wash cloth, soaped it up and washed his body all over. She then reached for the shower head and rinsed him off. He was loving it. How could he cheat on his beautiful queen? He looked down at her as she was bent down rinsing off his feet. He then took her puff brush and soaped it up with that wonderful smelling body wash. He took her hand and had her sit down on the shower bench. He kneeled and starts to wash her neck and runs the hot pink brush across her breasts which were hard. This turned him on. He pulled her up and put one of her legs on the bench. He gently began washing her pussy, which he couldn't wait to get in. He grabbed the shower head and rinsed her off. Monique went to put her leg down and he put it back up on the bench. He looked at her pussy and told it he was sorry.

"What are you doing?" She laughed.

"Apologizing to Sasha." He looked up

"Oh, she forgives you, now give her some attention." She pushed his head down.

Harmony put the keys in the door to her parents' home. It was quiet in the house. She walks in the kitchen to see if her mother had cooked anything, there was nothing. She walked through the house screaming her mother's name. She walked to the bedroom door but it was locked, so she went back in the family room to sit and wait for her mom. While she waited, she would just text Treasure to see how she was doing.

"WYD" She text

"Nothing HBU." Treasure replied

"At my moms." Her and Xavier in here fucking, Eww." She laughed.

"Aunt Mo, getting it in. Ha Ha." Treasure laughed

"I want to see you, soon" Harmony sent.

Monique and Xavier came into the family room. They were surprised to see Harmony sitting there. Monique gave her daughter a big hug. Xavier did the same. They were all smiles and touchy feely with each other.

Harmony thought that was so cute. She hoped one day Tristan would be like that with her.

"When did you get her?" Monique asked her.

"A few minutes ago, I was yelling your name. You didn't hear me huh?" She laughed.

"Don't be a smart-ass." She smacked her shoulder.

"You have to use it or lose it." Xavier told her.

"The two of you just made me sick." Harmony gave them a look.

The two sat down and looked at each other, then looked at Harmony. She was wondering like what is going on.

"What?" She asked them.

"We have something to tell you." Monique said.

"Are you pregnant?" She looked at them.

"No." Xavier said.

"Umm no." She looked at Xavier and rolled her eyes.

"I was about to say you're too old for that." She laughed.

"Actually, I'm not. I'm not even forty yet, so." She told her.

"Ok, then what is it." She looked concerned.

"Your dad is out of Prison and wants to see you." Xavier said.

Harmony was silent. Davon wanted to see her and Treasure. She didn't know how she felt about that. Would Treasure even want to see their dad? He really hurt everyone with what he did to aunt Keysha.

"I have to tell Treasure, that he wants to see us. How did he get out anyway?" Her face was twisted.

"Well I don't know how he got out, he didn't say. He also doesn't want to see Treasure, just you." She told her.

"Oh, hell no! If it's not the both of us then it's nothing." She yelled.

"You don't have to say anything else baby girl. I will take care of this." Xavier told her.

"No Xavier, please don't get involved with this." She told him.

"Too late, he should have never interrupted my family." He told her.

Harmony just sat back in amazement. How could they let that man out? She watches her mom try and convince Xavier not to have a confrontation with Davon. Harmony could care less what Xavier did to him. Xavier told Monique he would be back and to trust him. Monique sat down and began to cry. Harmony got up and walked over and sat down beside her and hugged her.

"It's going to be ok." Harmony said.

"It won't Harmony." She said.

"Why? Let Xavier whip his ass." She said to her mom.

"I slept with your dad today." Monique told her.

"Yeah, I heard y'all." She laughed.

"No, I mean Davon." Monique looked at her.

"Why would you do something so dumb mom? That man has ruined our life in so many ways." Harmony sat back.

"I walked in on Xavier fucking another bitch today at work." She began to cry.

"What? You didn't whip that bitch's ass." She asked.

"He never knew I was there, I went to tell him about Davon and I walked in on him. He has never seen me." She said.

"Mom you deserve better, but to sleep with Davon. Anybody but him." She said

"It just happened so quickly." Monique told her.

"It will be okay, mom." She hugged her.

"I hope Davon doesn't say anything. Me and Xavier worked out our shit today." She said to her.

"Yeah I heard." They both laughed.

"No, I'm serious Harmony." She looked sad.

"Mom, he's a convict and a liar. Xavier will not believe him and if he asks you. Lie about it. Hell, he cheated on you and who knows what else he has done. You good mom." She hugged her.

"What is that noise?" Monique asked her.

"Oh, I was texting Treasure." She said.

"Are you going to tell her?" Monique asked her.

"Yes, I have to." She said.

Harmony looked at her text to see what Treasure had sent her. She was nervous now, with the news she would have to tell her.

"When you trying to meet up." Treasure sent.

"I have to tell you something." She sent back.

"What?" She was nervous; please don't let her be pregnant by that boy. He is gay...

"Xavier cheated on mommy." Harmony told her.

"That bitch, she okay?" She asked.

"She good, but that's not the half of it." She took a deep breath

"What do we have to beat someone's ass?" Treasure said.

"Our dad is out of prison." She hesitated and pushed send.

****

Treasure turned around and looked at her mom. Keysha knew something was wrong. She stood up and walked over to Treasure. Treasure just showed her the text messages. Keysha was shocked and began to text back on her daughter's phone. She sat the phone down and walked away.

"I need you and Aunt Mo to come to this address, now."

16 SHIT JUST GOT REAL

Xavier is sitting at his desk in a daze. Asia is talking to him, yet he is not paying her any attention. His mind is on Davon. He leans back in his chair and turns it towards the window and taps his pen on the table. Then he jumps up and throws the stapler. Asia jumps up and is scared; she has never seen Xavier act like this before. Rosa runs in, with her hand across her chest. "Mr. Baptiste, are you ok?" Her voice was shaking. "I'm sorry Rosa, I'm fine." He told her. "Ok, boss." She shuts the door. Asia walked up behind him and wrapped her arms around his waist. He pushed her away. She looked at him in a confused way, they had just had sex yesterday and he acts like this. "Asia, that shit that happened the other day, will never happen again. You understand me." He told her. "Why? Did I do something wrong?" She asked him "No, it just ain't happening anymore. It's all business from here on out." Xavier explained to her. Asia realized she has lost again. Davon had told her that he wanted nothing to do with her. She knows now that he was just using her all these years and she wasted her life running behind a man, who never really wanted her. Now, here Xavier goes telling her the same thing. She was feeling angry, it was okay for him to fuck her at his leisure and now discard her like trash.

"Wow, so you were just using me?" She said

"Asia for real, today ain't it. You don't want this right now." He told her.

"I think I do." Asia said

"Ok, since I am feeling like I don't give a fuck. I will run it down for you. I fucked you when I wanted to because I could. I thank you for your pussy and so many others that allowed me to push my Benz, live in my big ass house and buy MY wife whatever the fuck she wants. If it wasn't bitches like you, with deadly mouths, I wouldn't be able to make a profit in the game of pippin." He told her.

"Really Xavier, I thought we were better than that." She told him.

"Well now you know we not, bring me the girls and your brother and I won't put your dumb ass back on the street." He shot her a look.

"Never that boss, you tried it." She told him.

"None of your smart mouth shit either. Let this be known to you, if you thinking about stepping to my wife. Think again. I will kill you on sight and not think twice about doing it. I'm going to let that shit slide. Just this once, but best believe I won't let it slide again. Understood!" He yelled and she jumped

"Understood." She said.

"Good. Now back to business. My niece is going to be starting here next week. I don't want her to know what's going on." He told her.

"Well what do you want me to tell her about the clients?" She asked.

"Nothing, tell her you do job placements. I don't want you to take her on any jobs. Make up some type of fake paper work for her to do." Xavier said.

"Ok, what's her name?" She asked him

"Treasure." He said.

"It couldn't be." She said.

"What?" He asked her.

"Nothing I was talking to myself." She was nervous.

"So, did you get the girls like asked for, and the two guys?" Xavier asked her.

"Yes, I have everything taken care of." She said.

"I need you to sit tight and I will contact you with further instructions." He told her.

There was a knock at the door and it was Blaze and no Marco. This was weird because they traveled in packs. She walked over to the beautiful painting of a black man, holding the weight of the world on his shoulders. Asia wondered if the girl Treasure was the same one she was impersonating. It couldn't be; she would have seen this girl by now. Considering she has seen Xavier's family. She turned back to see Xavier punching his hand. What were they talking about? The problem had nothing to do with her; she didn't want to get on his bad side today. He had said enough to her. "Hey Asia, we good here. Let's get up." He told her

"Ok, cool." She knew to get the hell out of there and she did.

Asia walked out and shut the door behind her. She waved at Rosa and headed to the elevator. Rosa wasn't sure what was going on, but she never asked questions. Rosa minded her business and was just appreciated all that Mr. Baptiste has done for her. Xavier and Blaze were walking out of the office. Rosa heard Mr. Baptiste saying he was going to learn today. What could he be talking about?

"Rosa it's your lucky day." Xavier said.

"Why is that?" She asked.

"Two days off early and with pay." He smiled.

"Are you serious boss?" She jumped up and hugged him.

"I am, go and enjoy your Friday." He told her.

Rosa once again, shut her computer down and grabbed her purse and headed to the elevators. Xavier and Blaze stood there until she got on the elevator. Both waving good bye to Rosa. As soon as the elevator doors closed, they looked at each other and headed to the conference room.

"That nigga give you and Marco any problems." Xavier asked.

"Naw, X, He's a straight punk." He told him.

"Well let's go deal with him." Xavier said.

Blaze opened the conference office doors, to let Xavier in. Marco was standing in front of someone sitting in a chair. Marco turned around and dapped up Xavier and Blaze. Once he moved out of the way. There sat a bloody, beaten Davon.

"Well player, you know who I am??" Xavier asked him

"No, man I don't." Davon said.

Xavier punched him in the face. Blood began to run from Davon's mouth and he thought he was going to die. How could Jug have this king of power?

"We have someone in common." Xavier told him

"Tell Jug, he didn't even give me a chance to home yet, I have only been home a little over twenty-four hours." He said

"I don't know any fucking Jug, but I do believe you know my wife Monique and my daughter Harmony." Xavier smiled at him.

He looked up at him out of the one good eye, because the other had been closed by Marco. Why would her husband bring him here? Did he find out that he slept with her?

"You mean my daughter." Davon said

"Naw, nigga I mean my daughter. You are going to leave my family alone and that would include Treasure." He said

"You're not going to keep me away from my daughter Harmony and as far as Treasure. She ain't my daughter." Davon told him.

"Yo, man you ain't shit. You know that's your daughter too. You fucked Monique's cousin and got her pregnant too. You going to deny those pretty green eyes you gave them." He asked.

"She's not mine!" He yelled

Xavier punched him in the face again. He snatched him up out of the chair. He punched him in the stomach. Davon was breathing hard. Xavier felt like he wanted to kill him. He threw him on the floor and started kicking him. Blaze ran over and pulled him off of Davon.

"Yo, X. Don't kill'em." Blaze said.

"Yeah man he will remember this beat down and stay far away." Marco said.

"He better!" Xavier yelled at him

"I'm not, that's my family." Davon said.

Xavier started to go for him again, but Marco and Blazed stopped him. He was going crazy and all he wanted was Davon to be gone.

"Yo, throw him out before I kill him." Xavier said.

Marco picked him up. Davon knew right then and there, if he was going to kill him, he would have done it by now. So he thought he would get up under Xavier's skin.

"Don't bring your ass around my family anymore." He told Davon.

"That's why I fucked her." Davon said.

"Fucked who?" Xavier asked.

"Monique, nigga. She came by yesterday crying and upset. So, I did what I always did. Take care of my baby." Davon started laughing.
"Oh really." He shook his head back and forth.

Marco and Blaze let Davon go and stepped away from him. Davon didn't know what was going on. Davon fixed his clothes and started towards the door. Xavier took his gun out from around his back. Davon froze in his steps. Xavier pulled the trigger twice hitting Davon in the head.
"Get this nigga out of here and clean up this mess." Xavier walked out of the conference room.

Xavier walked back to his office. Did Monique go see him yesterday? She told him that Davon had called her. He does recall her being upset yesterday. Davon had to be lying. He had taken care of the problem and his wife and step-daughter were ok. Xavier thoughts were interrupted by a phone call.
"Hey baby." Monique said.
"I was just thinking about you." Xavier said.
"All good I hope." She laughed.
"Of course, baby." He said.
"I wanted to check with you, Treasure wanted me and Harmony to spend the weekend with her." She told him.
"That would be nice; she's opening up to you." He said

"So you're okay with that, I need a break after this week. With Davon getting out of prison. Harmony was upset, that he only wanted to see her. Davon makes me sick babe." She said.

"Don't worry, he's a deadbeat and I'm pretty sure he won't be bothering you, Harmony or Treasure again." He told her.

"I hope so." Monique said

"By the way, you didn't go see him did you?" He asked

"No, I told you he called me and got the number from his mother." She lied.

"I couldn't remember." He was fishing

"So, see you Sunday. Stay out of trouble and be true to me." Monique said.

"Always, I love you." He said

"I love you too." Monique hangs up.

17 A SISTERHOOD CAN NEVER BE BROKEN

Monique was so excited to see Treasure. She had not seen her in months and just wanted it to be the girls. As she sat on the passenger side of the truck, she began to reminisce about her and Keysha. All the things Keysha did to make sure she was okay, to make sure she graduated from high school. She really missed her. "Keysha would be so proud of Treasure." Monique looked at Harmony.

"Mom, she sees her and all that she has accomplished." Harmony grabbed her hand.

"Look at me I'm hanging with the young girls this weekend." She laughed.

"But you're not young anymore." Harmony laughed.

"Oh be quiet." She hit her on the hand.

The next couple of hours they traveled in silence, listening to music. Just looking at the mountains and being on the winding roads, calmed Monique. She went back to that night with Davon. She had to admit his sex game, was a little better than her husband. The way he laid her down and climbed on top of her and kissed her neck. Biting her shoulders, and whispering how much he loved her. Monique knew that was a true statement and she had to admit she loved him just a little too. Davon had flipped her on her stomach and made her arch her back as he put his hard dick inside her.

"Mom, Mom!" Harmony yelled.
"Yes." She answered.
"We are here!" she yelled.
"Don't ever yell at me." She told her.
"I was calling you and you never looked over. What has you all smiling like that?" Harmony asked her.
"I wasn't smiling. Was I?" She felt hot.
They pulled up to the log house, it was gorgeous. The u-shaped driveway with the cobblestones and old timey well in the front was quaint. It was so peaceful, how the trees were blowing back and forth ever so softly as if they were singing a beautiful lullaby. Standing in the doorway was Treasure, looking so beautiful with her faux locs. She had on a pure white halter jumper, with her dreads in a turquoise and white head wrap. Davon had given both the girls those beautiful green eyes. Treasure looked at her Aunt Monique, what did she see, when she looked at me. Can she tell I'm hiding something from her? Her heart was pounding all hard, but she was so excited to tell them about her mom. She stepped out onto the porch and hugged them both.

"So, Auntie you ready to party with the youngins." She laughed.
"Oh you and Harmony got jokes." Monique turned around and started shaking her butt.

"What do you think you're doing?" Harmony slapped her on the butt.

"Forget her Auntie, you got this. Yes do that thing auntie." She laughed.

"Yes, do it Moe." Keysha said.

Monique stopped dancing. She couldn't turn around; it was like her feet were stuck to the porch. She knew that voice and it couldn't be her, could it? She looked at Harmony's face; she wanted to see what her expression was. Harmony had her hands over her mouth and she was crying. Monique began to cry, but still haven't turned around. Keysha put her hands on her shoulders and turned around. Monique could not believe it; Keysha was standing there with tears running down her face. She grabbed Keysha and hugged her so tight; she never wanted to let her go. Keysha felt the same way. In her heart Monique was her sister, not just her cousin.

"Come on Mo, let's go in the house." Keysha told her.

"Is it really you?" She touches her face.

"Auntie Keysha, what? How? I mean, I don't know what I mean."

"We will explain everything to you, let's just go inside." Treasure said.

Monique was holding Keysha's hand as they walked into the house. She looked around at this stunning home. Whose home was it? All this beautiful furniture, sectionals and beautiful paintings, fur rugs and a monstrous fireplace filled the family room. Monique sat on the sofa, Keysha walked toward the bar. Monique wouldn't let her hand go. Keysha smiled and kissed Monique's hand and she let it go. Treasure took Harmony to another room in the house so they could talk.

"What do you want to drink? Keysha asked her.

"Anything." She was in shock.

"Do you drink now?" She giggled.

"I do, smart ass." Monique said.

"What? I can't believe it."

"Do you have any wine?"

"Wine? Your ass is still bougie." Keysha told her.

"Well do you have some shot glasses and Ciroc?" She told her.

"Yes I do." Keysha started to laugh.

"What happened to you Keysha?" Monique asked her.

Keysha walked over to the sofa and grabbed her hand. She told her what happened in jail, when she took a girl under her wing that look and reminded her of Treasure. Monique found out how this girl betrayed her cousin and tried to kill her. Keysha told her how her daughter saved her life that night in the hospital. Monique was confused as to why she would not want her to know about all of this. Keysha then told her that she thought she was really going to die and she needed time to heal physically and spiritually before she could face anyone.

They started hugging and staring at each other because she could not believe Keysha was alive.

"Are you two finished crying?" Treasure said.

"Be quiet mouth." Keysha told her.

"Auntie I'm so glad you're ok." Harmony hugged Keysha.

"Me too, baby." She kissed her.

"So we good out here, I told Harmony everything. I hate keeping secrets from her." Treasure said.

"Well I think we all need to clear the air, right mom." Harmony looked at her mom.

"Really? Let's grab the Ciroc and shot glasses and head to the secret place." Keysha said.

"Secret place?" Monique asked her.

"Let's go, but can we bring some food, I don't want to get sick on my stomach?" Harmony said.

"Like mother, like daughter. Can't hold your liquor." Keysha laughed

Keysha grabbed some blankets and they headed into the woods. They came to a clearing area of the forest. Keysha had already had a fire pit, pre-ready. All she need to do was to start the fire. They all sat and laughed about old times. There was fried chicken, macaroni and cheese, cookies, biscuits'. They were just eating off napkins, because they had forgotten the plates and everyone to one side of the pan and dug in. They played the game have you ever and were taking constant shots. Keysha was so happy to be with her

family and not having to look over her back. Then
Monique blurts out what has been bothering her for the
last couple of days.

"Xavier cheated on me." She said. It was silent.

"Xavier your husband?!" Keysha asked her

"Yes." Monique wiped her face.

It was so silent in the woods, that you could hear the
leaves blowing back and forth. Everyone was just
staring at Monique. Harmony felt so badly for her
mother because she was herself in love with someone
she believed loved another. Harmony had no proof,
just a gut feeling. Keysha put her hands on Monique's
shoulder and squeezed it. Treasure never said anything,
just looked at the women she loved more than life itself
and knew it was time to get everything back in order.

"What you want to do?" Keysha asked her

"What do you mean? Crazy self." Monique smiled.

"Yeah, mom. Let's take over." Harmony said.

"Are you serious about taking over?" Treasure said.

"Ok, hold on before we make any plans to wreck shit."
Keysha said.

"Yeah hold on." Monique said.

"First, are you sure he cheated?" She asked

"I have the pictures to prove it." Monique told her.
Monique pulls out her phone and shows Keysha the
picture of Xavier having sex with a young lady from
behind. Keysha is stunned and her face reflects that.
She could not believe what she has just seen.

"Do you know this girl?" Keysha asked her.

"No. Why?" Monique looked puzzled.

"Let me see the picture." Treasure said.

Treasure grabbed the phone and looked at the picture and didn't recognize the person. Harmony took the phone and her mouth dropped and she put her hand over her heart. She had the same look on her face as Keysha did. Treasure and Monique did not what the hell was going on. Treasure stood in front of the fire and asked what was going on.

"This is Tristan's sister." Harmony said.

"Who the fuck is Tristan?" Keysha asked.

"He's Harmony's boyfriend." Monique said.

"I know this girl too." Keysha said.

"How?" Treasure asked.

"She's the one that tried to kill me." She said.

"That bitch is dead." Treasure said.

"Wait! Wait!" Monique yelled.

"Wait for what!!!!" Keysha yelled at her

"Mom he cheated on you and you don't know how long." She told.

"I hope you feel the same way about Tristan ass." Treasure said.

"What! I'm sure he knew nothing." Harmony defends him.

"He's fucking gay!" Treasure yelled.

Treasure and Harmony begin to argue back and forth. Monique and Keysha looked at each other and began to laugh. They reminded them of when they were younger. They were laughing so hard that Treasure and Harmony stopped arguing and wondered what they are laughing at. Treasure put her hand on her hips.

"What is so funny?" Treasure asked.

"Yes, I would like to know." Harmony chimed in.

"We used to act like that; I guess that is what sisters do." Keysha said

"Yes, sister." Monique grabbed her hand

"We are like sisters." She said.

"No we are sisters, I just have never told you." Monique said.

"What?" Keysha looked confused.

"Gerald is your dad too, I found out while you were in jail." Monique told her.

"Really." She hugged Monique.

"You're not mad." She asked

"No, I always felt like you were my sister, so this confirms it." Keysha said.

"What a fucking day?" Monique said.

"We are the craziest family, or sister, cousin loving selves." Treasure said.

"This is a dysfunctional sisterhood." Harmony said.

"Ok, with all that behind us. What are we going to do about the situation before us?" Treasure said.

"Let's find out what is really going on." Monique said

"How are we going to do that?" Keysha asked

"Treasure you start to work with Xavier on Monday, start digging." She smiled

"I got you." Treasure said.

"I will get closer to Tristan sister Asia, to find out why she tried to kill you." Harmony said.

"Her name is Asia?" Keysha said

"Yeah, what did she say her name was?" She asked

"Treasure." Keysha told her.

"That bitch! I'm going to get her."

"Calm down, we have to plan out whatever our intentions are and be careful." Monique told them.

"In nine months, everything should be good." Keysha said.

"Why nine months?" Harmony asked.

"You have to research, recruit and the react. Time, it takes time." She said

"What do you have in mind?" Treasure asked her.

"We need to have weekly contact or meetings." She said.

"Ok." Monique said.

"I've also contacted some old friends of Pamela's in Chicago. They will be able to help us with everything." Keysha told them

"Team take down on three." Treasure said.

"Except Xavier" Monique said.

"Tristan too." Harmony said.

"Yall just sad." Treasure told them.

"Look, let's see what happens after a couple of meetings okay." Keysha said.

"One, two, three." Treasure said

"Team take down." They all yelled.

18 BOSS MOVES

Treasure had been working for her uncle for eight and a half months and nothing has come about it. Xavier keeps his business completely under a tight lid. Blaze and Marco are true henchmen and there are constant secret meetings with Asia. Treasure has be trying to gain Asia's trust but with no success. Today she had an idea of how to get come out with her tonight. Treasure knocked on her uncles' door and waited to be Okay to come in. She looked at Rosa and smiled.

"Good afternoon Ms. Rosa." Treasure said

"Good afternoon, you look cute." Rosa said.

"You know I try Ms. Rosa." She turned around.

Marco opened the door and let Treasure in. Xavier was sitting at his desk and Asia was sitting across from him in a chair. Blaze was standing behind her uncle on his right side. It got silent as if she walked in on a big secret. She handed her uncle the report that he requested that she complete for him. It was a bull shit report and she knew it. Why for the last eight months she has just been plugging numbers into a spreadsheet? She smiled at Asia; inside she really wanted to kick her in the throat.

"The word around the office is it's your birthday Asia." Treasure said.

"Yes, it is." Asia said

"Well, happy birthday." Treasure smiled.

"Thank you, Treasure." Asia told her.

"I didn't realize it was your birthday." Xavier said.

"Yep, the big twenty-five." She smiled.

"Twenty-five, I would never have guessed that."
Treasure looked evil.

"Why is that?" Asia said in a smart way.

"What?" Treasure said.

Xavier stood up; because he knew Treasure had a temper.
Xavier walked around the desk, because Asia stood up.
Treasure was hoping she would step to her; she had
already had plans to pick up the paper weight and crack
her in the mouth with it. Xavier grabbed Treasure and
started hugging her. They looked at each other and
started to laugh. He knew the craziness that was running
around in her head. That's why he loved her so much
because she was just like him.

"You know what Asia; let's go out tonight, my treat."
Treasure said

"I don't think so." She sat down.

"Wow, really. You're going to do my niece like that."
Xavier gave her an evil look.

"That's okay unc, she too good to hang with me."
Treasure said.

"No, actually I'm not." She said.

"Okay, so meet up tonight." Xavier said.

"Yes, I will pick you up. Dress nice as you always do."
Treasure smiled at her.

"Will do." She smirked.

Treasure hugged her uncle and slapped hands with Blaze.
She walked out of the door and closed it behind her. She
leaned up against the wall and laughed to herself. She

had to calm herself because she almost screams "we got you bitch." Rosa was watching Treasure the whole time. "Are you okay?" She asked her.
"Yes ma'am." She told her.
Treasure turned around and walked back to her little office at the end of the hallway. It was now time to put her plan into action. She had a short amount of time to make it happen. Treasure needed to contact her mom. She has had eight months to get Asia and she was not going to let this opportunity. She grabbed her cell phone and put in a group text with her aunt Monique, mom and Harmony.

"My part is almost done, get the cabin ready. I will have her there around 8 Harmony make sure Tristan is there." She typed
"On my way to his house now, meet you." Harmony answered.
"Been ready." Keysha said.
"Team takeover." Monique typed.

Now that Treasure had gotten Asia to come to the cabin tonight, it was up to Harmony to get Tristan to come as well. She really wondered if he was gay. Harmony did not believe it. Her goal is to save her man and prove to the family that he was a good guy. She looked herself over once more before she knocked on the door. Harmony had on the purple dress he bought her and the black heels he loved so much. She took a deep breath and waited for Tristan to open the door. He opened the door with a little bit of a surprise on his face.

"I didn't know you were coming by today babe." He leaned in to kiss her

"Yes, I wanted to surprise you." She smiled.

"It's always a good surprise when you come through." He moved so she could come in.

The house was always so immaculate. There was never out of place, not even a jacket thrown on his sofa. She loved the décor, such clean lines. Harmony almost felt bad for sitting on the sofa. She motioned for him to come and sit next to her. She squeezed his hand. Tristan didn't know what to expect. He was glad she came over because he wanted to tell her it was over. He was in love with Marco and he needed to end it with her completely.

"Baby, I missed you." She said

"I missed you too, but we have to talk." He told her

"Talk about what?" She looked confused.

"About our relationship." He told her.

"What about it?" She began to look nervous.

He placed his hand on her ring finger and took a deep breath. Harmony got nervous; she started to think he was going to set a date. He gave her this ring almost a year ago. She was thinking, how she couldn't wait to throw this up in Treasure's face. Tristan swallowed hard and was about to just say it. When Asia bust in the door and starts cussing.

"Tristan you won't believe this shit, you know Treasure right?"

"I know Treasure, what about her?" Harmony was on the defense.

"Oh, Hi Harmony." She said nervously.

"Umm hmm, hi." She looked at her.

"Hey sis." He walked over to kiss her.

"So, what is it that you couldn't wait to tell Tristan about my cousin? I would definitely want to know that." She crossed her legs

"She invited me to go out for my birthday." She said.

"Oh and you pissed about that." Harmony asked her.

"No, no I'm not." She said it nervously.

"Didn't sound that way to me." Harmony leaned forward.

"Babe you always reading something, into nothing." He said.

"So where are you two going?" Harmony asked.

"I don't know." Asia spoke.

"Look babe, can we talk later. My sister is upset." He asked.

"Upset about what?" She looked at him.

"I'm not upset." Asia said.

"You right more like pissed and you don't want to go." Harmony said.

"Harmony cut the shit." He told her

"What?" She said.

"Tristan don't do that." Asia said.

"Yeah, you're right. I better leave." Harmony got up to leave.

"Harmony?" Asia called her.

"Yes." She said

"Why don't you and Tristan come too?" She said

"No. I don't think so." He said.

"I think it would be a great idea." She said

"Good." Asia said.

"Treasure and I will pick you two up at 8 o'clock, be ready." She kissed Tristan.

Tristan walked Harmony to the door and kissed her. He did not want to ever put his lips on her anymore. He just wanted the whole thing to be over and tonight it would. He turned around and leaned up against the door rubbing his head.

"I don't fucking like her Tristan." Asia said.

"After tonight we will be done with all of them." He said.

"You have the passports and did Marco transfer the money." Asia asked.

"Yes, this whole time Xavier thought he was using him, but it was us embezzling from him." He laughed.

"We may have to take care of them tonight, so I'm bringing my gun just in case, shit goes down." She said.

"Harmony is so in love with me, she wouldn't let anything happen to me." He said

"Let's hope so, let's get ready for this phony ass birthday celebration." She said

"Then off to the Bahamas tomorrow." He fist bumped her.

As Harmony walked to her truck, she started to feel like Tristan was defending his sister instead of me. It didn't

matter because once she becomes the wife; Asia would have to step to the side. She reached in her purse and pulled out her cell phone. She began to text Treasure.
"Team takeover." Harmony texted
"Yes, getting everything ready." She responded
"Guess who is riding with you?" Harmony told her.
"Who?" she asked
"Me and Tristan." She replied
"How?" Treasure asked
"OMW over now." Harmony replied.
"Ok, waiting." She said

****

Monique was looking at her eight month old big belly in the mirror and she was so happy to be giving Xavier a child. They had been together a long time and never had any children. Xavier was standing in the doorway looking at Monique. She was glowing, with no clothes on a huge belly, she was still gorgeous. He still didn't understand how it happened. The doctors told him he could never have children. This is something Xavier never told Monique; he knew she wanted more children. Monique turned around and smiled at him.

"Hey baby." Monique walked over to him
"Hey Mo." He leaned down to kiss her
"Hey Mo, that's what you call me now." She said

"What are you doing staring at yourself butt ass naked?"
He changed the subject.

"Enjoying being pregnant and giving my husband a
child." She smiled.

"You are getting big." He laughed.

"Xavier that is not funny." She hit him in the shoulder.

"I'm sorry Mrs. Thickems." Xavier laughed again.

"It feels so good to have a man in my life that is going to
be here for me. Not like Davon." She said

"Do we have to talk about that nigga?" He said.

"No, I'm just saying that, he tracks me down and then
begs to see his daughter and just now disappear off the
face of the earth." She said.

"He just trifling babe." He said and hugged her.

"His mother called me again today and asked have he
contacted me, it has been months since she got that letter
from him saying he was leaving and don't look from
him." She said.

"Is she trying to find him?" He asked.

"I told her I haven't seen him in eight months." She said.

"What you mean seen?" He asked.

"I meant spoken to." She clarified.

"Oh ok. We don't want any problems, do we?" He said.

"Shit that hurts." She grabbed her stomach.

"You okay?" He asked.

"No my stomach and back hurts." She said.

All of a sudden a gush of warm water ran down her legs.
Xavier and Monique both looked at each other. She still

had a month to go. Xavier began to panic, running around the room.

"Xavier calm down." She said.

"Ok, calm down." He said to himself.

"I'm going to get dress and I need you to drive me to the hospital." She said.

"It's too early for the baby to be coming." He said.

"It's going to be fine." She told him.

"You want me to call Harmony and Treasure." He asked.

"No, just take the packed bag and take it to the car." Monique told him.

Keysha was at the cabin sipping on some wine. She was so happy that she would finally get to confront the fake Treasure. She couldn't wait to see the look on her face. It was going to come to pass, that everyone was going to get theirs. Nobody knew that Keysha had been in contact with her mother's old lover from Chicago. They have been following Xavier, Asia and Tristan for months. She couldn't wait to tell everyone, all that she knows and it was a lot.

"Everything is ready Keysha." Sal told her.

"Thank you for all your help." She said.

"Not a problem, I owe Pamela everything. That was my true love right there. I will always take care of you." He said.

"I'm forever in your debt." She hugged him.

Monique was in so much pain and they were getting stronger. The doctor was on his way in to check her. She hoped he could stop the baby from coming she felt it was too early. Xavier was pacing back and forth. This was making Monique even more nervous.

"Baby please stop your making me nervous." She said.

"Mrs. Batiste, how are you?" Dr. Mason asked.

"Her water broke and she is in a lot of pain." Xavier answered.

"Babe he was asking me." She smiled.

"Oh, I'm sorry." He smiled.

"Yes, Doc everything he just said, I need some pain meds." She told him.

"Let me check you and then we can get the pain meds." He told her.

"That hurts." Monique moaned.

"Ok, we are having a baby right now. You are fully dilated." He said.

"Will the baby be ok?" Xavier asked.

"She's far enough where the baby should be fine." He said.

The nurse came in and set up the room for delivery. Dr. Mason put his scrubs on and started to instruct Monique on what to do. Xavier stood at the top of the bed behind Monique's head. He was excited this would be his first and only child. Then he heard the cry and the baby was here.

"It's a boy!" The doctor said.

"A son Xavier." Monique cried.

"My son." He smiled.

The nurses took the baby and were cleaning him up. The doctor was taking care of Monique. Xavier was so happy that he hadn't yet gone to look at the baby. Monique was all cleaned up and was ready to see the baby.

"We have a son." She said

"Yes babe we have a son." He said.

"Do you want to hold your son sir?" The nurse said.

"We have to name him babe."

The nurse handed the baby to Xavier. He was so happy, to see this beautiful bundle of joy. He had the most beautiful yellow skin and he had on a blue hat and wrapped up in a light blue blanket.

"I know what to name him." He said.

"What babe?" She said.

"How about Davon?" He said.

Xavier handed the baby back to the nurse and walked out of the room. Monique didn't know what was going on. The nurse is looking very confused. She walks over to give a now crying Monique the baby.

"Are you ok?" The nurse asked.

"I don't know." She said.

The nurse hands her the baby and Monique reached for him. She looks down at the baby and he looks up at her.

"He has the most beautiful green eyes." The nurse said.

"Yes, he does." She breaks down crying.

"Are you ok?" The nurse asked.

"Can you please just take him?" Monique asked her.

The nurse took the baby out of the room and to the nursery. Monique just cried and cried, she cried so much she almost threw up. Her phone began to vibrate and she thought it was Xavier. She knew he would not leave her. She looked and it was Keysha calling. Monique needed her to.

"Hello." Monique said.

"Hi sis, how are you?" Keysha asked.

"Not good." Monique began to cry.

The door slowly opens and it is Keysha standing there. Monique was so happy to see her. She didn't know how she knew that she was in the hospital. Xavier must have told her, Monique thought. Keysha walked over to her and hugged and kissed her. Monique held her tight.

"Are you ok?" She asked.

"You will never guess what's going on now? "Monique told her.

"Believe me I already know." She said.

"How?" Monique looked confused.

"Remember Sal." Keysha asked her.

"Yes, but I still don't understand." She said.

"He's been following Xavier, Asia and Tristan, even before you knew I was still alive." She told her. "Your sis is taking care of everything." And kisses her on the forehead.

There was a knock on the door and the nurse comes in with the baby all dressed and in a car seat. Monique looks at Keysha who appears to not be alarmed by it. Keysha hands Monique some clothes and motions her to get dressed.

"Ok, ok. What the hell is going on?" She slowly gets out of the bed still sore from her birth that was just hours ago.

"Do you trust me?" Keysha asked her.

"Yes, but what is going on." She asked.

"This is Gina and she is with us." Keysha explained.

"Ok." Monique looked confused and concerned.

"We don't have a lot of time; we need to get back to the cabin. I will explain everything in the car." She hurried her.

"But Xavier." She started to say

"I already know; we will handle him too." She said. Monique wasn't quite sure what was going on but she trusted Keysha. Keysha handles business and family is everything to her. So, without further questions for Keysha from her, she showers, gets dress and leaves the hospital with Keysha and Gina.

"Ok." Monique looked confused and concerned.

"We don't have a lot of time; we need to get back to the cabin. I will explain everything in the car." She hurried her.

19 REDEMPTION

Xavier is driving top speed in his crisp white Range Rover. He could not believe it, Davon was telling the truth. That he had slept with Monique. He was done with Monique, Harmony and Treasure. He never wanted to see them again. He was happy that he had killed Davon, if he couldn't be happy, no one would be. Xavier just wanted to be with someone tonight. He knew that there would be girls working tonight at the hotel. Marco and Blaze were already there, making sure everything was going right. He had already been sleeping with Therasa, a beautiful Italian goddess. He called her up.

"Yes, Xavier." Therasa said.
"Oh, you just knew it was me huh." He laughed.
"Of course, papa'" She said.
"I need you tonight, right now." He said to her.
"Ok, I'm already at the hotel, room 305." She said.
"On my way." He said.
"I will be waiting on you and whatever it is it will be okay." She comforted him with her voice.
"Yeah, I hope so." He told her.
"How far away are you?" She asked.
"About ten minutes." He said

Xavier ended the call and was headed to the hotel. He was relieved to be with someone tonight that really didn't require anything from him. Xavier knew he was the boss and so did she. First thing tomorrow he was putting that whole lying ass family on the street, baby and all. It was the old Xavier from now on, if it didn't have to do with his business, money or bitches making money for his business. He didn't have any soft feelings about anything else. Xavier was relieved that he had kept Monique out of the real nature behind his business, because if she knew he would have to kill her and anyone connected to her.

Treasure is looking at the clock and it is seven thirty and the time was ticking. Harmony was in her room getting dress. She hoped that after tonight that Harmony would be okay. She was almost positive that Tristan was gay and using her. Treasure really wanted everything to go as planned and not get over anxious and punch Asia in the face or anything like that. She walked to Harmony's room to see what was taking so long. She was just standing in the mirror smiling. Treasure thought, "What the hell is she smiling for?"She looked down at her watch and they needed to go.

"Hey crazy, let's go." Treasure said.

"Yes, but you think we are doing the right thing." She asked.

"Look we have to get our family back on track and yes we need to do this." She grabbed her hands.

"Ok, let's go, but I think you're going to be surprised by my man." She smiled

"I hope so Harmony. I really hope so." Treasure said. Treasure knew Harmony would not be right after tonight. She would have to be there for her cousin. Harmony was not street smart at all; she leads with her heart and not her head. Everything in soul tells her that Tristan is not who he says he is. Tonight, they would both find out. They shut the doors to the jeep and headed out.

"Tristan hurry up, they will be here in a few minutes." Asia yelled.

"Ok, I'm coming." He said

"Remember, don't say anything about the break up until we get back here." She told him.

"I will try, are you bringing your gun." He asked her.

"We won't need it." She smiled.

"Okay, I don't think that is a good idea, I just have a feeling." He told her.

"So, you want to tell Xavier we pulled a gun on his daughter and favorite niece." She reminded him.

"You right about that, I wasn't thinking." Tristan said

"She just text me, they are outside." Asia said

"Let's go." He breathed hard.

****

Treasure was sitting out front and had just text Asia that she was outside. She sent another text to her mom to let her know that they were on the way to the cabin. Her heart was beating so fast. She had to tell herself to calm down. Harmony sees Asia and Tristan walking towards them and gets out the car so that she and Tristan could get in the back. Asia was wearing this cute sparkly cocktail dress and Tristan was dressed in black jeans and a button-down shirt with a dress jacket. He looked so handsome to her.

Tristan could tell by the way Harmony was looking at him, that she really loved him. He had to admit she did look gorgeous. He loved when she had a bun on top of her head and the little red dress, with the strappy heels. He walked up to her and gave her a hug and a kiss on the forehead. This took Harmony by surprise.

"The birthday girl." Treasure said.

"Yes, here I am." Asia smiled.

"Happy birthday Asia." Harmony said.

"Thank you." She said.

"Hi Treasure." Tristan said.

"Hi you look really nice." She said.

"So where are we going?" Asia asked.

"Before I tell you about our night, let's take some shots." She said.

"I don't really drink like that and you're driving." She said.

"Come on sis, live a little." He said.

"Come Asia, I don't drink either, but I am willing to celebrate with you tonight." Harmony said.

"I won't take my shot until we get to the surprise celebration spot." Treasure said.

"Well that leaves us." Tristan said.

"Ok what you got." She asked.

"Jell-O shots and Ciroc." Treasure said.

"One of each for me." Tristan said.

"I will try the Jell-O shot." Asia said.

"And the Ciroc, live girl!!" Treasure told her.

"Just give me the jell-o shot." Harmony said

"I know a red one, with the gummy bears in the bottom." Treasure laughed

Treasure gave everyone a shot of Ciroc and two jell-o shots. Asia only asked for one but she gave Tristan and her both two. Harmony took her gummy jell-o shot and down it. Everyone put their seat belts on and Treasure pulled off. Harmony asked Treasure to turn up the music. The liquor had Asia so relaxed she asked for another jell-o shot and so did Tristan. Harmony didn't take anything else. She needed to be sober for the night. As for Tristan he had already passed out and we were only thirty minutes into their hour and a half or so ride.

"Oh my gosh, can you turn the air condition on!"I'm so hot." Asia asked.

"Sure, are you okay?" Treasure asked

"I'm feeling really dizzy and weak; I think you may have to take me home." She slurred.

"No I don't think so Asia." She looked at her.

"Why not, where are we going?" She yelled.

"If you don't shut the fuck up." Treasure said.

"What was in those drinks?" She asked.

"Oh, just a drug to heavily sedate you, I want you to meet someone." Treasure said.

"Sis!" Tristan yelled.

"Baby, she is passed out in the front." Harmony said.

"She drank too much." He laughed.

"She did baby. I love you so much." Harmony said.

"I really don't love you Harmony; I've been trying to tell you that." He said then passed out.

Treasure looked in the rear-view mirror. She had heard what Tristan had just said. Harmony was looking out of the window and was wiping tears from her face. She hoped that tonight would revealed the truth to Harmony but she didn't want her to be in pain. Now that the medicine had taken effect on Asia and her brother. She could now contact her mother. This whole thing was about to come to an end.

"Harmony text my mom and tell we should be there shortly." She said.

"Ok." Harmony said

"Are you alright?" Treasure asked.

"I'm fine and I don't want to talk about it." She told her.
Treasure didn't say anything the rest of the ride home.
Harmony just stared out the window the whole time,

never saying a word. She did once look over at Tristan and he was leaned up against the window snoring.

****

Xavier parked the truck and jumps out. He could not wait to get in the room with Therasa and let her love him down. As he entered the beautiful hotel, that had a huge crystal chandelier hanging from the ceiling. The first person he sees are Marco and Blaze. They walk up to him and shake his hand. He didn't want to talk business until after he had sex and relieved some stress.

"What up E?" Blaze said.

"Nothing." He said.

"Is something wrong, everything here is good." Marco told him.

"I just came to take care of some business and then I'm leaving." He told them.

He walked to the elevator and pushed the third floor. He stepped off and room 305 was to the left and at the end of the hall. He realized as he was walking to get the room key from the front desk clerk. He reached the door and knocked on it. Therasa came to the door wearing a black panty set. She grabbed him by his shirt and pulled him in and began kissing him. His dick was so hard, he felt like he was already about to cum. He pushed her back into the room and shut the door.

"I want you so bad." He kissed her.

"I could tell when you called me that you were stressed out." She told him.

"If you only knew." He told her.

"Well tell me over this shower I'm about to run for you. Come with me." She said.

"What do you have up your sleeve?" He smiled.

She took him in the bathroom. She reached into the shower and turned it on for him. As she was bent over he was looking at her huge thick ass. She came towards him and started to undress him, Xavier stepped out of his shoes. He allowed Therasa to undress him. He wanted to be pampered. He got into the shower it felt good on his back, he just wanted the day to be over. She pulled the shower curtain back and handed him a drink in a clear crystal glass. He downed the drink and asked for another one and she got it. Little did Xavier know while he was in the shower, that the hotel was being raided.

"Don't take all day sexy." She said.

"I'm on my way baby." He told her.

Xavier got out of the shower feeling a little drunk. He didn't understand this, he could drink a fifth of vodka and feel nothing. He wondered what kind of drink she gave him. Therasa was laying across the bed with the rope, because he loved to tie her up. He stumbled towards her. She sat up in the bed and looked at him.

"Babe are you ok?" She asked.

"What did you give me?" He asked her.

"It was just vodka, just like you like." She told him.

There was a vicious knock at the door. They both looked at each other. She got up and went to the door to see who it was. He wrapped the towel around himself and motioned for her to open the door. It was a frantic Marco and Blaze. She let them in.

"X we have to go, the feds are here." Blaze said.

"What? All shit, let's go." He was slurring.

"What's the matter with you?" Marco asked.

"He's been drinking; I will help him get dressed. So, you can get him out of here." She said.

There was a hard bang at the door. Everyone was silent. Therasa looked at X, she was bent down trying to put his pants on. The next thing was one guy busting in the door, holding up a badge. She jumped up and pushed her back up against the window. Everyone was still.

"So, can we help you." Xavier asked him as the room continued to spin.

"I don't think so Mr. Baptiste." He said.

"Oh, you know my name." He said to him.

"I came for you, the head nigga in charge." He said.

"You came by yourself that wasn't very wise of you." Xavier told him.

Marco and Blaze pulled out guns and had them pointed at the federal agent. For the life of him he couldn't get sober enough to do anything. Therasa grabbed some clothes and pulled her gun out. Xavier stumbled to get dress. The federal agent didn't even look concerned at all.

"Looks like today isn't your day." Xavier said.

"I think I will be fine." He said

"No I don't think so bro." Blaze said.

"So, either way you're not leaving this room alive, sorry." Xavier said.

"You think so, huh." He said.

Blazed cocked his gun. Xavier looked at the federal agent and gave him a smile of victory. Shots rang out. Xavier jumped back. Marco had shot Blaze in the head. Xavier could not believe that he had betrayed him. He didn't know how to get of here. He still had Therasa holding him down and he knew she would die for him.

"Marco, really nigga." Xavier said.

"Yes, X. Meet my Uncle Sal." Marco said to him.

"And my Uncle Sal too." Therasa looked at him with the gun pointed at him.

"Ok a family affair. What do you want to be a part of my business?" He said.

"No thank you sir, we are going to take all your money and assets. That you will sign over willing, I would hope." He laughed.

"You will have to kill me first." He said.

"Whatever it takes because as of now, you have no business." Sal said.

He didn't know how he would get out of this one, he looked on the floor and blaze was dead, brain matter all over the floor. While he was trying to figure a way out of this, Therasa hit him over the head with her gun. She knocked him out.

"Uncle Sal what are we going to do with Blaze." Marco said.

"I got this. There is nothing to worry about." He said.

"I'm glad you came when you did, I did not want to sleep with him one more time." She said.

"You two just get him to the cabin. It's time to end this." Sal said.

Keysha has gotten Monique upstairs and well rested. The baby was sleeping and Gina was taking care of them with meds, checking the baby. Sal had really come through for her and she knew she was forever indebted to him. Everything was coming to a head and she couldn't wait for it to be over. She heard a vehicle pulling up. She wasn't sure if it was Treasure or Sal. She walked to the door and stepped onto the porch. It was Treasure and Monique. She could see Asia and Tristan sleep in the truck. Treasure sees her mother and puts the truck in park and turns the car off. She opens the door and gets out with Harmony right behind her. As they walk up to meet Keysha. Two big guys walk past them, that they had never seen before. They open the doors and started shaking Asia and Tristan to wake them. They finally got out the truck looking tired and confused. They had guns drawn and they knew better to make any sudden moves.

"Get out of the car." The guy said.

"Where are you taking us?" Asia asked him.

He put the gun to her head and she got out. He pointed towards Keysha. As they were walking, Asia couldn't make out the face of the woman. Treasure and Harmony stood next to Keysha. As she got closer she recognized who it was and she became scared. She knew what Keysha was capable of. Her brother looked at her but didn't know what was going on. The guy pushed her in the back to walk up the stairs. They were walking past she tried to put her head down and look the other way but Keysha stopped her.

"Well hello Treasure, I mean Asia correct." Keysha asked her.

"Keysha where do you want these two?" He asked.

"Take them to the spot." She smiled.

He marched them back down the stairs and headed to the woods. Asia knew it was payback time and she would not be coming back out of the woods alive. Tristan was hoping that Harmony would save him. He would plead for his life and love her the way she wants him to.

"Is my mom here?" Harmony asked.

"Yes, she is and your new little brother." She said.

"Brother, wow that's pretty cool." Harmony said.

"Hurry up go see the baby." Treasure said.

Harmony knocked on the door and opened it. Monique looked up and seen it was her daughter. She began to smile, she was relieved to see she was okay. Harmony walked over and kissed her. She looked at her brother who was sleeping.

"Mom he is beautiful." She said.

"Just like you were." Monique told her.

"You ready for this." Harmony asked her.

"Too late to turn back now, and it's something's that will be revealed that you need to know." She told her,

"I don't need any more surprises tonight." She told her.

"What happened?" She asked her.

"While Tristan was drugged, he told me he doesn't love me." Harmony said.

"He will be getting his shortly. He has been lying to you the whole time." She told her.

"What do you mean?" She asked.

Monique started telling her everything Keysha told her. She told her about how Sal had been watching everyone. Tristan had been in a relationship with Marco for about a year now, how Xavier really was running a prostitution ring in the hotels, how he had been cheating on me through this whole pregnancy with Therasa, his niece, and how Xavier had killed Davon. Harmony sat down on the bed, she could not believe it. Her dad was dead and her step dad killed him. Her heart was starting to harden, she wanted all of them to die. Keysha came to the door to let them know it was time to handle this business.

"Are you ladies ready?" She asked.

"Yes." They both said.

"Okay. They just took Xavier down to spot. Here are the signed papers of all his assets, banking accounts and off shore accounts. It has a little blood on it but it is signed." Keysha told her.

"Monique, are you okay, do you want to take something?" Gina asked her.

"I'm still numb from earlier, I think I will be fine." She said.

Treasure peeked her head in the door; she looked at Harmony and could tell she was visibly upset.

"Team takeover are you ready." She asked.

"Yes." The all said.

Xavier was sitting on the cold ground, blood dripping from his nose and could barely see. Marco had closed his right eye. He didn't want to look up at Asia, who was also sitting on the ground with hands tied. Tristan just kept looking at Marco, wondering was he going to save him. He was in love with him. Marco never looked his way. Sal stood in front of all of them.

"You were all brought here by the same people and here they are." He said.

Monique, Treasure, Keysha and Harmony emerged from the woods. The light from the fire was reflecting on their clothes. Tristan was trying to make eye contact with Harmony. He starting yelling out her name. She walked over to him and stood over him and looked him in the face.

"Don't let them kill me baby, I love you. I thought we were getting married." Tristan begged.

"You don't remember this but in the car when you were drugged you talked and talked. You know what you told me. How you and Marco were going to rob Xavier and move away. How you never loved me and I was just a cover." She looked at him.

He didn't say anything; he looked at Asia; who wasn't crying at all, just sitting. Then Monique stood in front of Xavier, Treasure and Keysha stood in front of Asia, with Harmony still in front of Tristan. They each told them the reason they were going to die.

"Before you start, I have to say something." Sal said.

"Please go ahead." Keysha said.

"Loyalty is everything." He said as he shot Marco in the head.

"NO!" Tristan said.

Marco had plans on trying to save Tristan and Sal got word of it so he felt as though he couldn't trust him.

"Without trust, it won't work." He said.

"Did you swab his mouth, Sal?" Monique asked.

"Yes, Gina is on the test as we speak." He told her

"I'm not going to beg you not to kill me." Xavier told her.

"We are going to speak our truths, then pull the trigger." Keysha said.

"You killed my daughters father." She said.

"You fucked my aunt's husband." Treasure said.

"You tried to kill me in jail." Keysha said.

"You used me and broke my soul." Harmony said.

They all pulled out their guns. Three shots rang out and Xavier was shot in the head, Asia was shot in the chest and the head. Harmony was still holding her gun, she couldn't do it.

"Please Harmony, don't." he begged.

She just stood there looking at him. She thought about how she looked at bridal dressed, he allowed her to love him. When his intentions were to run off with another man. She looked at Treasure and pulled the trigger and Tristan fell over.

"Is everybody ok?" Sal asked

"We will be just fine." Keysha spoke for everyone.

"We will clean this mess up, please go back up to the house." Sal said.

They walked in silence. The night had been crazy. As the leaves crackled under their feet, they locked hands. Nothing was spoken, but redemption had been made. No one knew how life would be now. It was an opportunity for a new start.

****

It had been six weeks and everything was finally back to normal. Treasure and Harmony had moved to California. Treasure was going to school to become a lawyer and Harmony was going to school to become a psychiatrist. Monique and Keysha kept the cabin in the woods and lived together until they decided what their next move would be. Monique had millions of dollars from Xavier. There was no rush to do anything.

"Hey ugly, you have mail." Keysha said.

"What is it? She asked.

"It's the DNA results." She handed to her.

Monique was nervous. Either way her son would not have a father who was living. It was just for her peace of mind that she had him tested. She opened the letter. Keysha couldn't tell by her facial expression what the results were. Monique got up from the kitchen island and walked outside.

"Where are, you going?" She asked

"I'm going to the spot." She said.

Keysha didn't ask who the father was. She knew that Monique would tell her when she wanted to. She watched Monique slowly disappear in the woods. Monique never came out to the spot. It's a day that she wanted to forget. She finally made her way to the clearing. She walked over to where Xavier was placed.

"Well hello Xavier. I just wanted to talk to you. I wanted you to know I wish we could have worked it out. I wished I never slept with Davon and maybe none of this would have had to happen. I got the results today on the baby." She said out loud

She took the folded-up letter and placed it on his grave. She was so overcome with emotions she began to cry. She bent down and said a silent prayer.

"Miracles do happen and I promise to bring your son out here to see you as much as I can." She said.

ABOUT THE AUTHOR

This is Andrea Lige-Saddler second urban novel. She is the
business owner called RISK & RISE. Andrea's company
consist of youth empowerment and teen reduction programs.
Her plans are to reach as many teen and young emerging adults
as possible. To give them the tools to be successful in life,
when there is no one to cheer them on.